The
ICE
HOUSE

The ICE HOUSE

MONICA SHERWOOD

LITTLE, BROWN AND COMPANY
New York Boston

Copyright © 2021 by Monica Sherwood
Interior art snowflake © ngaga/Shutterstock.com; falling snow background © Lina_Lisichka/Shutterstock.com

Cover art copyright © 2021 by Tom Clohosy Cole. Cover design by Jenny Kimura. Cover copyright © 2021 by Hachette Book Group, Inc.

Little, Brown and Company
Hachette Book Group
1290 Avenue of the Americas, New York, NY 10104
Visit us at LBYR.com

First Edition: November 2021

Little, Brown and Company is a division of
Hachette Book Group, Inc. The Little, Brown name and
logo are trademarks of Hachette Book Group, Inc.

The publisher is not responsible for websites (or their content)
that are not owned by the publisher.

Library of Congress Cataloging-in-Publication Data
Names: Sherwood, Monica, author.
Title: The ice house / Monica Sherwood.
Description: First edition. | New York : Little, Brown and Company,
2021. | Audience: Ages 8–12. | Summary: As a worldwide, extreme
freeze continues, Louisa's family, neighbors, friendships, and
schoolwork are all affected, leading her to build an icehouse in the
yard to escape
Identifiers: LCCN 2020050440 | ISBN 9780316705349 (hardcover) |
ISBN 9780316705325 (ebook) | ISBN 9780316705332 (ebook other)
Subjects: CYAC: Winter—Fiction. | Family life—Fiction. |
Apartment houses—Fiction. | Icehouses—Fiction.

Classification: LCC PZ7.1.S5163 Ice 2021 | DDC [Fic]—dc23
LC record available at https://lccn.loc.gov/2020050440

ISBNs: 978-0-316-70534-9 (hardcover), 978-0-316-70532-5 (ebook)

Printed in the United States of America

LSC-C

Printing 1, 2021

For Rose Hyland McGuinness, my nana

One

"*It might start* melting by next Friday," Dad said. "Sergeant Cole got a tip from someone at the National Guard."

Mom forced the hard edge of her shovel into a mound of frozen snow.

"I'll believe it when I see it," she said over the crunch of metal against ice.

"Maybe they're right this time," I said.

Dad looked up at me from the almost-cleared front walkway to our building. "Maybe is right."

He'd been predicting the end of the Freeze about once a week ever since the worldwide phenomenon had started in the middle of September, six months ago. New snow had continued to fall nearly every day since, piling higher and higher, until thick layers of ice seemed to cover everything. It was hard to imagine it ending anytime soon, but I knew Dad was trying to stay positive for us, so I didn't mind playing along with him.

Will, my six-year-old brother, kicked his booted foot against the ledge Mom had made along the sidewalk while shoveling—she'd piled the snow high because there was nowhere else for it to go. What was once the front lawn of our apartment building looked like a bunny-hill ski slope.

"And then I'll get Louisa's old bike, like you promised, right?" Will asked.

"Yes, then you'll get Louisa's bike," Mom said.

She lodged her shovel in the snowbank, her black hair falling in front of her eyes from the force of the effort.

I didn't want to shovel anymore, either.

When the Freeze first started, Dad and his friend Brian, our downstairs neighbor, had volunteered our families to help Mr. Yu, our elderly landlord, shovel the sidewalk and front path of our building. There were five apartments in our building altogether. The other tenants were pitching in as well; we rotated weekends.

At first, it had been exciting—I'd never had a reason to shovel before—but now, after months of this never-ending weather event, it was exhausting. Lifting my arms sent a dull ache up to my shoulders, and my eyes were stinging from the cold.

Mom's fair skin was sprinkled with golden freckles; her cheeks popped bright pink from the cold. She shook her hands out and turned, looking out onto our street.

The sky was ominous and full of thick clouds, like marshmallows stuck together. My favorite trees had died, and instead of cherry blossoms, there were icicles hanging from the branches. Their gray trunks taunted me like zombies.

Right past the trees, Brian, his wife, Alesha, and their son, Luke, were trying to break up some of the thick ice coating the sidewalk. It was weird to think about how Luke had been my best friend when we were little kids. Now, even though we were in the same sixth-grade class and our parents were super close, we weren't.

Brian's voice carried through the wind. He was

singing something, but I couldn't hear the words. Luke seemed to be dancing along, and Alesha giggled as she watched.

Even though I rolled my eyes at Luke's weird moves, I couldn't help but wish my family still goofed around like his. Mom didn't crack jokes anymore, and since Dad was a first responder—a firefighter—all he ever seemed to talk about was the Freeze.

Brian noticed me staring at them and waved me over. He was Dad's age—they'd been best friends ever since high school—but the dark brown waves of hair spilling out from under his red beanie made him look a lot younger.

Alesha's eyes lit up as I trekked through the snow toward them. She had an oval birthmark on her left cheek and the prettiest curly eyelashes I'd ever seen. Today she wore her long dark hair in tight braids that she'd tucked into the collar of her lilac puffy coat.

"Lou—back me up here," she said, once I was close. "This morning Luke was complaining about how we don't know when the Freeze is going to end, but I'm telling him he should look at it like an adventure. We're living through this historic moment. You'll get to tell your kids about it one day, right?"

Our frosted-over apartment building, the shut-down and lonely-looking bodega on our corner, the streets slick with black ice: I tried to picture them on the front of a history textbook.

It didn't seem anything like the history we learned about at school—the Great Depression or the civil rights movement. We were just stuck inside, watching snow fall and wondering when it would end.

At his mom's question, Luke stopped dancing and huffed. "If I was living through history," he said, "I'd want to live through the seventies. Not now."

"Why the seventies?" I asked. To me, the seventies seemed like a million years ago. It made me think of the old, sort of orange pictures from when Mom and Dad were really little kids—the ones where Nana still had long, wavy brown hair and wore bell-bottom jeans.

"Because in *Rodrigo and the Moon*, it's 1970. Space exploration was just beginning," he said.

Of *course* Luke was talking about Rodrigo, his favorite graphic novel series; it was all he ever talked about. Rodrigo was an average seventh grader who'd been obsessed with the moon landing. A year after the landing, in 1970, he'd woken up on the moon. He had to find his way back to his family, and every book in the series was about a step on his quest. I'd never read it, and the more Luke talked about it, the less I wanted to.

"I'm tired of this part of history. I'd want to live in the future, where hopefully it's warmer," I said, brushing off Luke's answer and turning to Alesha.

"You've got a point there," she said. I knew Alesha hated cold weather; she'd grown up in Jamaica and always missed the heat.

"Here, warm up like this, then." Luke jumped up and down, smiling with satisfaction. He looked pretty silly.

Brian was whistling now and wedging the edge of his ice pick into the crevice where the cement would have met the lawn.

"What's that song?" I said, taking a step away from Luke and toward Brian.

"It's one I'm writing right now. . . . I think I'll call it 'The Coldest Day.'"

Brian was a musician, the lead singer and guitarist of his own band. He played music Mom described as *folksy*. His voice was warm and comforting, even when he strummed his guitar fast and loud.

"Let's hear it," I said. I loved listening to Brian sing, even if it was a song he'd made up on the spot.

"Hey, spring! Did you forget to come around?
Why are there no flowers in the ground?
I love snow as much as anyone,
But will the shovelin' ever be done?"

Mom, Dad, and Will stopped shoveling at the sound of Brian's voice. They walked over to us, standing behind me in the snow. As he sang, I kept time, tapping my foot to the beat. It crunched against the snow, that crisp first-bite-of-an-apple sound.

"If you love ice-skating, it's the day for you.
If you love snowmen, you know what to do.
If you have a snowblower, it's your lucky day.
If not, pray it ends by May!"

When he'd finished, Brian bowed dramatically. We clapped, but our thick gloves muffled the sound so you could hardly hear it over the wind whistling past us.

"Nice, Bri. It's no 'Lifeguard Blues,' but close," Dad said.

"What's 'Lifeguard Blues'?" Will asked.

"When we were teenagers, we'd lifeguard in the

summer. And you know, when you're a lifeguard you spend a lot of time sitting up on those tall chairs and watching everyone else have fun in the water, and you're so hot. Just baking in the sun. So Bri wrote a song about it."

"Sing it, Brian!" I said.

"You'll have to wait until my next concert. I don't have it in me to give 'Lifeguard Blues' the love it deserves."

"Come on, Dad," Luke said.

"On my birthday, when the Freeze is over, we're going to have a big party on the beach, and I'll do a private friends-and-family performance of 'Lifeguard Blues' then, in honor of summer."

"Dad just said it's gonna end next week," Will said.

Mom ruffled Will's reddish hair. "Let's hope so, bud," she said, her voice tired.

"What, you aren't having fun shoveling?" Brian said, peering down at Will. "Why don't you see if you can jump higher than Luke?"

"Uh, I *know* I can!" Will said, and he leapt up, like he was trying to reach one of the icicles hanging off the tangle of dying tree branches.

"There you go," Brian said, and Dad chuckled.

I wasn't convinced by Brian's birthday party promise. It was March now, and his birthday was at the end of June—it was hard to believe there were only a few months separating us from a snowless summer.

"When do you think it'll end?" I asked, looking up at Luke.

Even though I was exactly two months older than him, he towered over me. "You heard my dad. He thinks it'll be done by his birthday," he said. He took off his fogged-over glasses and rubbed at the lenses with the end of his scarf.

"Right. But do you believe him?"

"What, you don't?" Luke tilted his head, the pom-pom of his hat flipping to one side.

"I wish I did," I said.

"Don't worry. He knows what he's talking about."

It was hard for me to believe Brian, or my own parents, teachers, newscasters—anyone—after the world had stopped making sense.

Ever since the middle of September, we'd been living in a state of global emergency. On the news, we saw people all over the world struggling to cope with the unexpected snow. We watched videos of families in Brazil having snowball fights, explaining their confusion over the four feet of snow filling their streets in the summer, and their struggle with the delay in delivery of shovels and snowplows. At least we *had* shovels—some places weren't used to snow at all.

In our own neighborhood, stores closed, and a curfew was put in place. We had to order groceries and wait days for delivery as food trucks arrived less frequently. Mom and Dad froze all the food they could to make it last.

It became too dangerous for school buses to drive on the roads coated in thick ice, so we were stuck inside all day, meeting for class over video call. Just to walk around outside safely, we had to wear these boots with thick grips, the kind mountain climbers used.

Every night on the news, we heard more reports of car accidents on black ice, trucks swerving on highways, snowplows getting stuck in the middle of roads. Important people—politicians and doctors and celebrities—were given safety escorts on snowmobiles to get from place to place.

And then there were Dad's unbelievable stories: doors freezing over, trapping residents inside their buildings; heavy snow caving in people's roofs; hail cracking windows. He was always working double shifts, on call to handle emergencies I didn't like to think about.

Now, as we watched Dad and Brian try to knock icicles off the gutter with one of our shovels, I tried to shake my worry away. Our dads snickered as they took turns attempting to gain traction on the tall snowbank for a good angle to knock the icicles down.

"I'm the snow king!" Brian called to us from on top of a huge pile of snow lining the wall of the building; he waved the shovel like a scepter in his hand. Dad shook his head, cackling, and turned back to the gutter. When his metal shovel collided with the thick row of icicles blocking the gutter, a sound like glass shattering crackled across the yard.

I watched, mesmerized, as Dad smashed row after row of icicles along the front of the building.

"They're just going to have to do this again next time," I said.

Luke, rubbing his gloved hands together, said,

"Yeah, but it *is* kind of cool. It's like a battle with the elements: Will the ice attack our apartment, or will we eventually be victorious?"

My life wasn't a video game, and our apartment building wasn't the scene of some battle in a quest. If it was, after 180 days of the Freeze, it seemed like we were headed toward defeat.

Two

The next morning, I sat in the window seat at the end of our hallway while my class had our remote Morning Meeting video call.

Ms. Lee, my homeroom teacher, taught us Language Arts. She was intimidating, even over video. Her commanding voice made me question my own, so that I felt less certain whenever I had to speak in class.

"Remember," she was saying, "scientists can tell us their *hypotheses* about the Freeze—but right now, they don't have definitive facts about causes, solutions, or when it will end. Their theories and predictions are based on a number of factors: Earth's orbit, sunlight measurements, rates of ice melting..."

I ignored the rest of her speech as I watched snowflakes slam against our windowpane and melt. Ms. Lee had already told us this a thousand times; I wanted a real explanation, even if it was bad. Even if we were destined for ten thousand years of the Freeze, and I'd never swim in the ocean or catch fireflies or smell a blooming rose again, at least I'd know the truth.

"All right, Louisa, you're up."

I jolted at the sound of my name.

For our current events unit, everyone had to share a news story from the past week. The stories always ended up being about the Freeze, since that was all anyone seemed to talk about anymore. Some reports were more interesting than others, especially when kids brought up competing theories. Like last week, Millie and Jamal had both given reports on the recent scientific discovery that sunlight measurements in the northern hemisphere had stopped dipping and had plateaued. Millie's report said this was a good sign: It suggested we weren't entering a rapid ice age and the Freeze was gradually going to end.

But Jamal reported that the ice sheets the Freeze had caused—and that climate scientists had been studying—had shown no signs of melting. He said this suggested that the Freeze was the beginning of an unprecedented continuous climate trend that could potentially last over a thousand years.

By the end of Jamal's presentation, Millie looked upset.

"Sorry, Millie," Jamal said, and shrugged, like he was correcting her.

Ms. Lee intervened. "These are both theories—hypotheses. Scientists are still doing research around these findings." She rubbed her eyes as she spoke, like maybe trying to understand it all herself gave her a headache.

"Jamal and Millie showed us all a really important point today: One fact can be interpreted in two totally different ways, which is why we have to really consider the information we take in and make our own informed opinions about it."

I'd found the story I was going to present while I was reading about this group of scientists who hypothesized that the Freeze was a rapid-onset ice age. If this was true, massive regions of the world were going to become totally uninhabitable as ice sheets spread. Scientists who believed this theory were working with architects and engineers to figure out a way to use technology to create habitable ice structures. They were studying igloos to explore how the Inuit had built homes out of snow for centuries.

So far, they'd determined that some things were really important: building with old, crunchy snow instead of fresh powder; ensuring the snow was the same thickness throughout the structure. The architects were trying to figure out a way to build with the materials available to them; I'd had the same idea in Makers Club. As club president, I'd proposed we build a sustainable model of a city out of recycled materials for this year's Marvelous Metropolis competition.

I took a deep, rattling breath and fumbled for the unmute button so that I could start presenting; I didn't want everyone to know how nervous I was.

"So, the article I wanted to share with everyone is about building."

I stared at my classmates' little faces in the square boxes that lined my screen. With everyone muted, it felt sort of like I was talking to myself.

"If the Freeze is permanent, engineers and architects and scientists will have to figure out a way to make buildings out of the snow and ice. This article talked about a team of experts working to come up with possible ways to build safe structures out of snow. I had a connection to this idea, I guess, because in Makers Club we try to solve problems with what we have available, too."

My voice sounded shaky; I wondered if bringing up Makers Club made me seem a little nerdy.

"Nice choice, Louisa. Maybe some members of the club have more specific questions for Louisa about the article?" Ms. Lee said.

"Do you think they'll be able to build highways for cars, even with the ice and snow?" Nellie, one of my best friends, asked. "How would people get around, and transport all the materials and stuff, if the roads are still ice?" Nellie, Priya, and I had been pretty much inseparable since the end of third grade, around the time I stopped hanging out with Luke as much.

I didn't have an answer. I looked at Ms. Lee and felt my palms getting sweaty.

"Th-that's a good question," I stammered, after a

silence that felt painfully long. "Maybe with sleds? Or trains, if they treat the tracks with some chemical or something so that they don't ice over?"

"There are some risks there," Andre said.

"Well, how do *you* think they'd transport materials?" I shot back, my voice sharper than I'd meant it to sound.

"Maybe helicopters? Cars feel too risky at this point, but maybe there'd be some sort of invention involving wheel traction?" he said, seemingly unbothered by my snapping.

I should have thought about these questions before my presentation. As Andre continued posing possible solutions, I felt more unprepared, and I began to tune him out. In the corner of my screen, in one of the little boxes of faces, I saw Priya reading a book; she wasn't even paying attention.

After Andre stopped speaking, there was a pause where I wondered if I was supposed to answer him. When I didn't, Ms. Lee said, "Okay, well, thanks, Louisa. Great share. Make sure you post the link to the story in our classroom chat."

I mumbled a thank-you and turned off my microphone. My attention drifted out the window in front of me and to our backyard, where there was so much snow someone could build a structure without having to transport *any* materials at all.

~♋

When our class was finally over, I closed Dad's laptop with a sigh of relief. I was about to return it to the desk in Mom and Dad's room when I heard a shriek, and then a loud smashing sound.

"Will!" Mom shouted.

I abandoned Dad's laptop on the window seat and sprinted to the living room.

Mom stood by the tall armoire in the corner, her fingers pressed to her lips. The armoire's glass doors were open and Will was sitting on the floor, shards of ocean-blue glass littering the hardwood.

He peered up at me like a startled deer.

"Oh, Will," Mom said, quiet now.

"What happened?" I whispered.

"I was taking the vases down from that shelf to inventory them, and...I put them down on the coffee table. He just—he slammed right into it," she said, rubbing her eyebrow. "You know, I tell you not to run in here. I tell you that all the time."

"But I wasn't running!"

"He could have gotten... You could have gotten really hurt, Will. There's a reason we have rules... and now... it's... That was *Nana's*. The first thing I ever made for her—and she kept it her whole..." Mom took a seat on the couch, resting her head in her hands. Her hair covered her face like a curtain, but I could tell she'd started crying from the way from the way her shoulders shook.

I stared up at the empty space on the armoire shelf where Nana's blue sculpture had lived. When we'd cleaned out Nana's house a few months ago, Mom had taken it off the mantelpiece above the fireplace and held it close to her chest. When Dad noticed, he'd handed her another sheet of bubble wrap to protect it. On the drive home, she'd held it in her lap just to be extra careful.

Will was frozen like a statue. "Come," I said, holding my hand out to him.

∾

Our bedroom wasn't even a real room until I was five, when my parents had a wall put up that sliced right through the living room. Now Will and I shared a tiny room with an ugly old pipe in the middle; it whistled and clanged as heat steamed through it.

Will sat down on his bed, resting his head on his knees.

"I didn't mean to break anything," he said.

"I know."

"She's so . . . mad."

"I think she's just sad, really," I said.

"Why is she always so sad now?" From the whine of his voice, I knew it was a complaint, not a real question.

I picked at my cuticle, fraying off the side of my bitten thumbnail.

"She'll get better soon," I said. This was probably a lie, but it was a lie I told myself every day.

"But Nana will still be dead. So, how?"

"Once the Freeze ends, and, you know, things go back to normal, and she can go back to her studio, and summer comes, she'll feel better."

I wanted her to be the way she'd been before.

Whenever we'd visit Mom at her studio, she'd been the opposite of how she was acting now: buzzing around, examining a work in progress like a puzzle she was trying to solve; excitedly asking James and Rasheen, sculptors who rented the studio across the hallway from hers, for their opinions on a new piece; singing along to the music she blasted as she worked.

"You don't know that," Will said.

"You're right. But I hope so," I said.

Will sighed and flopped his head down on his pillow.

"Don't think about it anymore, okay? Accidents happen."

"Uh-huh," he said.

I wished I could take my own advice, but thinking of the shattered glass on the floor felt like a headache in my heart.

⌒

When I went back to the living room to help Mom clean up, she was on her knees, sweeping the broken glass into a dustpan like Cinderella.

"Can I help?" I asked.

Mom didn't look at me. "No. I don't want you getting cut on any of it."

"I can just pick up the bigger pieces," I said.

She sighed.

"Fine. Careful around the edges, and put the pieces in that box there," she said, pointing to a cardboard box on the coffee table.

The glass shards clinked against the metal dustpan with each of Mom's sweeps. I searched for pieces that were pretty big. I found a curved piece of blue glass the size of my palm on the floor. The sides were smooth, not sharp—and I slid it into my back pocket before Mom could see. Then I placed a few smaller pieces in the cardboard box as she'd instructed, trying not to make any noise at all.

After a few minutes, Mom's silence started to make me wonder if she was mad at me, even though I hadn't broken the sculpture. "Why were you taking the things out of there, anyway?" I said, mostly to see if she'd answer me.

"I'm selling all of it."

"What?"

"I'm not making new pieces right now, so I have to

sell the old ones. At least until I figure out what's next for me."

"Why?" I asked.

"*Why* what?"

"Why can't you make new pieces? The glass studio's only a few blocks away. You could walk there."

"I don't want to talk about this right now," she said, standing up.

"I'm just asking."

"I'm not going to do glasswork anymore. At least not for a while." She emptied the pieces from her dustpan into the cardboard box.

"Why not?"

"Because it's a very time-consuming, costly process that you have to be really passionate about to do well, and I'm not right now."

I nodded, unsure of how I was supposed to answer.

"Were you really going to sell *Teardrop*?" I asked. That was what I'd named Nana's sculpture years before, admiring it from the piano bench in her sunroom one afternoon.

"No. I was just going to dust it. It was the only one I was going to keep," she said, and then she picked up the cardboard box and carried it out of the living room. The pieces of glass rattled inside the box like a rain stick.

We didn't talk about *Teardrop* again, but I took the curved piece of glass out of the pocket of my jeans and hid it in the back of my bedside table drawer so that I could look at it whenever I wanted.

Three

The following afternoon, we had a remote Makers Club meeting. Mr. Rojas, our club moderator, was nothing like Ms. Lee. He never made me feel nervous to speak up, and he wasn't always lecturing us the way she was. Instead, he asked us a lot of questions—sometimes hard ones—that led to discussions and debates. *And* he drove a Vespa to school before the Freeze, and had his eyebrow pierced, which I thought was very cool.

I did like getting a chance to talk to him, but these remote meetings weren't the same as our in-person meetings. Nellie and Priya were on the call, but neither of them said much of anything. When we had meetings in person, the three of us always sat next to one another. I felt lonely, looking at them through the screen, wishing we could be together. As I listened to Keisha share a model of a playground structure she'd made out of Q-tips, and Diego showed us a needle-point of a skyscraper he'd made with his grandma, I felt frustrated; *I* was club president, and I hadn't made anything since the Freeze started.

"Before we wrap up, I have an update on the Marvelous Metropolis contest," Mr. Rojas announced. "We'll have to make changes to our entry. Instead of the sustainability solution we agreed on in September, all entries must pivot to solving a single question: How could a metropolis survive, grow, and eventually thrive under the conditions of the Freeze?"

I couldn't believe it. I'd been the one who'd proposed back in September that our focus be sustainability. This contest was just one more thing the Freeze had ruined.

"I know this is a change," Mr. Rojas went on, "and that can be frustrating, but it's also a chance to brainstorm how you might fix something right now, something that's a major problem in the present, instead of focusing on the future. So, does anyone have thoughts on how we'd modify our plans for the model?"

When no one said anything, Mr. Rojas moved a little closer to the camera. "What about you, Ms. President?"

"Well," I said, trying to sound less disappointed than I felt, "before, our project was really focused on what materials we would build with, and how we could make sure that the materials used would conserve resources but also last a long time. I think with the Freeze, those materials aren't as available, so first we'll have to decide what materials we'll build with instead."

"Well, there aren't a lot of options. I think it's just snow...and ice. So that's decided," Jamal said.

"Right," I said, "but we have to think about the problems that would come with that—like how would they make houses or schools or hospitals out of snow that would be warm enough for people to stay inside?"

"Let's pause right there," Mr. Rojas said. "Because I think *that* is the fundamental question we'll have to answer if we want to create a winning solution."

He was silent for a few seconds, and when he continued, he sounded thoughtful. "Before our next meeting, I want you to think about two things. First, a possible solution for building a school of snow and ice. Second, and this might be more important, think about the biggest challenge the Freeze has caused for *you*. Coming up with solutions for those challenges, the ones that impact your lives most, could give our metropolis an edge."

Everything about the Freeze was challenging. I couldn't pick just one thing.

~෨

That weekend, Mom made this chicken stew for dinner that tasted a little coconut-y and smelled like feet. Dad had gone to Costco weeks ago with some of the other firefighters in the truck, and they'd bought chicken in bulk to freeze. Mom kept coming up with unusual concoctions to make the chicken taste different, but I was sick of it. I had a feeling my parents were, too.

Mom picked her plate up off the table and put it in the sink. "I called the studio today. Let them know I'm not renewing my lease," she said, her back to us.

I watched Dad's jaw tighten.

"Gracie, you sure?"

"Yes," she said, squirting dish soap into the sink.

Dad's eyebrows wrinkled up like fuzzy caterpillars.

I looked from him to Will, who was scraping his left-over chicken off his plate and into the garbage in a hurry. He'd earned extra screen time this week, and I knew he wanted to get back to his tablet.

"But what if, when all this is over, you need to find a different studio? It could be tough—this one's so close. We could hang in there a little longer," Dad said.

Mom shrugged and picked up the rest of our plates, even though it was usually one of my chores to do the dishes after dinner.

Dad caught my eye and nodded toward the living room. He wanted to talk to her alone.

I stood up, but just then there was a loud knock at the door. Dad rushed to answer it.

Luke was standing in our doorway in his pajamas, the lenses of his horn-rimmed glasses looking cloudy. "Mike?" he asked, his voice higher than usual, like he was nervous.

"Hey, Luke. How's it going?" Dad sounded casual, but we all knew it was strange for Luke to show up like this at night.

"My mom told me to ask if I could stay here for a while?"

"Yeah, of course. Come on in," Dad said.

Luke stepped inside, barefoot, a lost look in his eyes.

"Everything okay, Luke?" Mom asked.

"It's my dad. We just found out that he was leaving the grocery store on First Street and a heavy tree branch that had iced over fell and hit him. My mom is going to the hospital to meet him."

"Hit him *where*?" Dad said, suddenly in work mode, his voice urgent and commanding.

"Outside the grocery store. Oh. I mean. On his head? I think? The person who called Mom said she'd called 911, and an ambulance took him to the hospital."

I looked at Mom. All the color had drained from her face. I knew she was thinking of the phone call she'd gotten from a stranger a few months ago, the lady who'd told her Nana was going to the hospital. I couldn't think about that day—that phone call, and Mom's face crumbling like an avalanche—without my stomach sinking.

"Did your mom leave yet?" Dad asked.

"She's still getting ready downstairs." Luke gave me an embarrassed look. "She's crying."

Mom looked at Dad, and they talked with just their eyes, in a way I kind of hated because I felt left out. Whatever they were saying, I could tell it was bad.

"Sit tight," Dad told Luke, and he grabbed his coat and slipped on his boots. I watched the worry crawl across Mom's forehead in wormy wrinkles.

After Dad left, Mom waved Luke over to the couch, and Luke obeyed, taking a seat beside her. She wrapped her arms around him and hugged him tight.

"You want something to eat, Luke?"

It seemed like a strange question. Luke looked really upset, not hungry. I knew that even if he was, he wouldn't have wanted chicken stew leftovers—no one would.

"No, I'm okay," Luke said.

"I'm going to go make some hot cocoa for you, then," Mom said, and she got up and walked to the kitchen.

I didn't know what to say to Luke once Mom was gone. I knew I should say something kind, something to make him feel better, but I couldn't remember what it had been like when we were friends, only a few years ago.

I got up and sat next to him on the couch, careful to leave space in between us.

"I'm sorry," I said.

He stared at the floor.

"He'll be fine," I said, but I felt like I'd said something wrong, because Luke just shook his head. So I added: "My dad says he helps people who have things fall on them, like branches, or store signs, or scaffolding, almost every shift. And most of the time, the worst they get is a broken arm or leg or something."

"A lot of people *aren't* fine when something falls and hits them, though," Luke said. His lips started wobbling. "My mom was crying a lot."

I thought about telling him that sometimes my mom cried a lot, too. But it felt like a secret I had to keep for her.

Just then she walked back in and put two mugs of hot chocolate down on the coffee table, filled to the top with whipped cream, which she usually didn't let us have.

"You'll stay here with us tonight, Luke," she said.

"Thanks," he said, eyeing his mug of hot chocolate.

Mom sat down in the armchair next to us. She

was wearing blue old-lady slippers that had been Nana's. I'd wanted to laugh the first time I saw her wearing them.

Luke was staring at Mom. "Your mom died because she slipped on the ice, right?"

Mom looked stunned at the question, and Luke made a face then like he hadn't meant to ask it at all.

Mom never talked about how Nana died.

She reached for Luke's hand. I watched her squeeze his fingers with her own. "She did." Her voice was soft like dough, and I watched Luke's eyes water.

"But she was old," I added.

"She was old," Mom repeated. She looked at me like I'd hurt her, even though I hadn't meant to hurt her at all.

∽

Luke and I stayed up watching reruns of *The Office* until way after my usual bedtime. Except for the occasional snicker at a joke, we both stayed silent.

I found myself watching Mom more than the TV. She sat in the chair beside our couch with her jaw clenched tight, her nail-bitten fingers drumming against its arm, her phone screen flashing on every other minute or so as she checked for updates that never came.

A little after midnight, Mom turned off the TV. "Okay. I think it's time we get some rest," she said, but the three of us stayed in our seats.

I'd assumed we'd have heard from Alesha, or at least Dad, by now. I knew that if Brian were fine, Dad would have texted Mom to tell Luke not to worry.

Mom exhaled, her voice sounding sad instead of tired. "Let's get you settled in Louisa's bed, Luke. She'll bunk with me tonight." Mom rested her hand on Luke's shoulder and led him down the hallway toward my room. "I made up the bed with new sheets for you, but I'm going to grab some extra blankets in case you get chilly," she said, hurrying down the hallway toward our linen closet.

"Thanks, Gracie," Luke said, and he hovered in my bedroom doorway.

"At least Will's snoring doesn't sound too bad tonight," I said.

"Oh. That's okay," Luke said, like he didn't hear it at all.

"Seriously, sometimes I roll him over onto his side to see if it'll make him stop. So if he gets loud, just come get me. I'll roll him over or make him sleep on the couch," I said.

"I'm used to it. My dad snores loud. I can hear it even from my room," Luke said.

I heard Mom close the closet door and knew I'd have an excuse to say good night in a few seconds.

"I wish my dad had texted us an update," I whispered.

"My dad's probably joking right now with him, teasing Mom for making such a big deal," Luke said, but the cheerful tone in his voice sounded forced, and when he met my eye his smile faded.

"Your mom is shushing them for making noise while other patients are trying to sleep," I said.

Later that night, curled up in Mom's bed, I painted a picture in my brain: Alesha shaking her head, a little annoyed but mostly entertained by Brian and Dad, who were doubled over with laughter while waiting for the doctors to tell Brian he could go home.

～૭

When I woke up the next morning, Luke was gone. I told myself that Brian was home, that Luke was downstairs listening to the story of his dramatic accident.

I walked down the hallway to the kitchen and saw a familiar brown bag sitting on the table. Dad had brought me a bagel: cinnamon raisin, toasted, with apple cream cheese. Sometimes, on Saturdays, Dad trekked to the bagel store a few blocks away. We almost never got takeout anymore, because it was often too dangerous for delivery people to travel, so bagels felt like a special treat now.

I didn't even take my bagel out of the bag, though. Mom was on the phone in the kitchen, and I didn't like the heaviness of her voice, her words quiet and clipped. I'd told myself that everything would be fine when I woke up, but I could still feel last night's tense energy in the air. The apartment felt eerie.

I crawled onto the couch in the living room and turned on the TV to drown out the ominous drone of her phone call, putting on a new episode of a show I'd started watching called *The Marina*. The show was about a group of teenagers who lived in a sunny seaside town. It was really mostly about the couples on the show, which I didn't care about, but I liked seeing the characters wearing summer clothes and hanging out outside the way we had before. I didn't like the show as much as Nellie, though, who'd been the one to tell me to watch it.

Ten minutes into the episode, Mom walked into the living room. I could tell Brian wasn't okay just by looking at her. She sat down next to me, and I paused the TV. "That was Alesha," she said, gesturing to the phone in her hand. "Brian's...he's not doing too good."

I picked at my cuticles.

When Nana died, I remembered wishing Mom had told me that Nana had gone to Florida on a permanent vacation, so I could have imagined her lying out on the beach or playing cards with her friends, instead of knowing she was dead. I was getting that same feeling now.

"They have to run some more tests, because sometimes when you hit your head, your brain can get injured and swollen. Until it has time to heal, it seems that he has memory loss."

I let out a breath I hadn't realized I'd been holding in. Having memory loss wasn't the same as being dead—his memory could get better. "What kind of things can't he remember?"

"Well, for now, it seems like he can't really remember people. He's confused," Mom said, fumbling with the sleeve of her sweater.

"*What* people?"

She took a long, loud breath. "Everyone: Alesha, Dad, Luke."

Of course, this was impossible. Brian was smart, and he still seemed like a kid half the time; old people lost their memory, not people Dad's age.

"The doctors are saying it's very possible that it's temporary. These things can happen sometimes with brain injuries. They're saying we have to wait and see."

"How do they even know? Maybe he's just confused and tired from hitting his head," I said. "Maybe he just needs to rest."

"I really hope so," she said, but as I searched her eyes, their deep blue glowing in the morning light, I could tell she thought it was permanent. "In the meantime," she said, blinking and looking down at her fingernails, "I really want you to be nice to Luke, okay?"

"Mom," I said.

"I know you aren't as close as you used to be, but he's a nice kid, and he's really going to need a friend right now."

"I'm always nice to him! I was nice to him last night!" I reminded her. I'd genuinely wanted to make Luke feel better. It wasn't like I *hated* him or anything; we just didn't fit together the way we had when we were little. "He's just kind of . . . intense," I said.

"Well, intense isn't bad! It means he cares about things," she said.

"He's always talking about *Rodrigo and the Moon*. I don't know what to say to him about it. He's always doodling pictures from it on his books at school. It's like I could bring up any topic to him, and he'd bring it back to stupid Rodrigo."

"You used to be such good buddies. Remember when we all went camping that one summer?"

"It was a long time ago," I said, biting my thumbnail. I'd been eight on that trip: four years ago. That was probably the last time I'd hung out with Luke for longer than the few hours we sometimes spent together when our parents had a family dinner party or barbecue.

"I think it would be good for *both* of you to have

someone your own age to hang out with," Mom said. "And he's just downstairs."

"I promise I'll be extra nice to him when I see him," I said. She gave me a look like she wasn't sure she was satisfied with my answer.

She left when Will started calling for her from the kitchen. I stared at the frozen TV screen—*The Marina* was paused on a beachfront scene, as a group of teenagers biked past an ice cream store on the boardwalk. Before the Freeze, a boardwalk hadn't seemed like a fantasy destination. A trip to the ice cream store had never been risky. On *The Marina*, it was still normal.

I wanted to go there, to the scene I saw frozen in time. Maybe Brian's brain was like this—paused, waiting for someone to hit play again.

Four

In the days after Brian's accident, Mom and Dad did everything they could to make Alesha's life easier. She spent every day at the hospital, leaving home early each morning and coming back after dark each night. She took a special shuttle that the hospital provided for safe transportation.

Dad visited Brian every day, too. He didn't talk about these visits afterward, but I had a feeling that the way he stretched out on the couch and closed his eyes as soon as he got home meant they didn't go well.

Luke spent most nights that first week with us. I tried to be extra nice to him in front of Mom, but I could tell she'd started to understand what I'd meant when I said that all Luke talked about was *Rodrigo*. One night, over dinner, he recounted one of his long and elaborate theories on the secret symbolism of book five to us, despite the fact that none of us had even read book one. I caught Mom covering a knowing smile with a forkful of macaroni.

∾

That Saturday, Brian had occupational therapy for the morning; Alesha was staying home, and Mom wanted to keep her company.

After I'd gotten dressed, I stood behind Mom as she rang the doorbell to Alesha and Brian's apartment. I hadn't seen Alesha since the accident, and while Luke had spent a lot of the past week in our apartment, Mom and Will's constant talking made it easy for me to stay quiet. I'd avoided saying anything to Luke about Brian since the night of the accident, and thinking about having to do it now made me feel queasy.

It reminded me of how at Nana's wake, she'd been laid out in a coffin at the front of the room in the funeral home. I couldn't look at her face close-up for more than a second: Her skin looked puffy and pulled, like the dough of a piecrust. I'd twisted my hands together, staring at her from a few feet back.

Halfway through the wake, Luke had shown up with Brian and Alesha, wearing a suit. He'd given me a little wave and even tried to smile at me, but the corners of his mouth were shaky, and when his eyes found Nana, the lenses of his glasses fogged up. Even though we weren't really good friends, seeing him then had made me feel a little better.

I took a deep breath, and as the door creaked open, my stomach tilted.

Alesha leaned against the doorway with her arms crossed and her braids dangling over her sky-blue sweater. She exhaled slowly, and I thought of the yoga lessons she sometimes gave Luke and me when we were younger. *Inhale—exhale*, she'd instruct, moving into downward dog seamlessly while I clumsily extended my leg too far off my mat and onto Luke's. Later, I'd repeat her words in the mirror, trying to channel the peaceful softness of her voice, the gentle rhythm of her Jamaican accent, but I never could.

"Alesha," Mom said, her voice heavy. Alesha's tears overwhelmed her face, like a tidal wave hitting the calmest beach. Mom pulled her into a hug, and Alesha sobbed, resting her head against Mom.

"I know," Mom whispered.

I decided I didn't have to stay there watching, so I swung past the two of them and wandered down the hallway to Luke's bedroom. The apartment felt too quiet. Whenever I'd visited before, there always seemed to be some music playing. Now it felt empty.

Right next to Luke's door, there was a picture hanging on the wall. It was a younger Brian onstage. The glow of the lights hit his hot-pink shirt, the green of his eyes bright as he took in the packed crowd in front of him. I stared at the photo, wondering how Brian could have forgotten a moment like that.

∽૭

"It's Louisa," I said, knocking on Luke's door.

"You can come in," I heard him say.

Luke looked small sitting on his bed, wrapped up in the same planet-covered blue blanket he'd had since he was a little kid.

"I was watching *Rodrigo*," he said. His voice sounded hoarse, like he hadn't used it in a long time.

"Oh," I said.

"You can come watch with me, if you want," he said.

Rodrigo and the Moon had been turned into a TV show. I'd seen bits and pieces of it before dinners at their apartment, and I wasn't into it.

I stared at Luke for a few seconds, trying to think of a polite way to say no. I knew how disappointed Mom would be if I came out of Luke's room right away. Alesha might think I was being mean to him, too.

"Okay," I said.

I climbed onto Luke's bed and he moved over to make more space for me. I noticed that his glasses had a lime-green lining on the rim.

"I like your glasses," I said.

"Thanks."

"I meant to say that when you got them."

"They're pretty old," Luke said.

"Oh."

"This is the third episode. Do you want me to go back to the first one so you can catch up?"

I was beginning to really regret agreeing to this, but I didn't want him to feel bad. "Oh. Well, maybe you could just explain what I missed."

"Okay," he said. He seemed a little happier at this suggestion. He pressed play on his laptop, and I decided not to complain when he restarted the episode from the beginning.

We watched three episodes before Luke turned it off; it felt like a long time had passed. "So, there are some important differences between the graphic novels and the series," he explained. "I kind of wish they'd gone more by the books, because it takes me out of it a little bit when they change things."

"Oh."

"Do you like it?" he asked, a hopeful look in his eyes.

"I guess. What do you like about it so much?" I said.

"I like the different missions he has to accomplish. And I like trying to figure out clues. After you read each book in the series, on the last page there are all these hints about the next book that you have to decode, to let you know what the next part of his mission will be."

"That *is* cool," I said, and I remembered then that even when we were really little, Luke had loved puzzles. We'd spent lots of rainy days working on them together.

"But I don't know—obviously, at the end of the book series he's going to figure it out, right?" I said, pulling at my cuticles.

"Maybe what's happening to Rodrigo's kind of, you know, what's going on with my dad," Luke said. He was very still beside me. "Like, Rodrigo is out in space, and he *wants* to come back home to his family, but he has missions to complete before he can. Maybe my dad has to do something, like a mission, before he can come back to us—something to help him get his memory back."

"Yeah," I said, but I didn't really understand how the two were related. "Maybe it is like that."

Neither of us said anything for a while. I wondered if I should leave.

Then he said, "My dad doesn't know who I am. My mom, either."

We both knew I knew this. I felt uncomfortable having to talk about it now, after a week of ignoring it. "I'm really, really, really sorry," I said.

I looked at him and was suddenly so sad that something so horrible had happened to someone so nice. Luke had let me come into his room and sit next to him on his bed, even though I hadn't really been a friend to him in a long time. If he'd shown up at my bedroom door, I wouldn't have wanted him there.

"I know it'll come back, though. His memory, I mean," he said, his voice so convincingly optimistic that I kind of believed him.

"Of course," I said, hoping my voice sounded as certain as his did. "Yeah...he'll get better soon."

Luke nodded, like this was a sure thing, but the only thing I knew for sure was that trying to find the words he needed to hear made me feel like I was in over my head.

Five

The heat in our building had this funny smell, a mix of our neighbors' apartments swimming through the vents to us: Alesha's spices, Mr. Khan's minty cologne, Mrs. Owusu's evening coffee grounds, and sometimes, when we were very unlucky, broccoli from someone's dinner.

It overwhelmed me that night, after my visit with Luke. I sprawled out on the living room floor beside Will, who was thumping his feet up and down. While surrounded by the stifling heat smell and Will's *thump-thump-thumpity-thump-thump*, I was trying to watch *Supermarket Sweep*. I never knew the answers, but watching it reminded me of Nana—it was her favorite show. Whenever we watched, we'd all call out our own answers over the contestants and make silly comments that made it more fun.

Tonight, though, Mom and Dad weren't watching—they sat behind us on the couch reading something on Dad's phone.

The room felt heavy, and I couldn't sit there anymore. "Anyone want some hot cocoa?" I asked my parents.

"No. I'm okay," Mom said. Dad didn't even answer, his eyes still glued to his phone.

"I do!" Will shouted.

I looked down at him. He was drawing this really detailed spacecraft on a piece of Mom's expensive drawing paper. She'd never let me use it before, and I wondered if he'd taken it without her knowing. I decided not to press him on this, though—I'd be nice.

"Fine. Come," I said.

The kitchen was colder than the living room. The window over our sink was old and drafty. The Freeze had been too much for it to handle. Dad had put in a request with the super to have it replaced months ago, but we were still waiting.

Will sat at the kitchen table watching me as I

made our hot chocolate. "Remember the snowball fight we had with Brian and Alesha and Luke?" he asked.

"Yes," I said. It had been months ago.

"Think we can do that again soon?"

I wondered what Mom and Dad had told Will about Brian. Sometimes, like now, he looked at me like there were answers he needed from me that I didn't have.

"I'm not sure," I said. I hated the heavy look he gave me then.

The microwave beeped, and I switched our mugs out. "Careful. It's hot," I said, setting his mug down in front of him.

"Can I have those big marshmallows?"

"Sorry. There aren't any left," I said.

He huffed. "Well, then I don't want this," he said, his cheeks flushing pink.

"Why can't you just say thank you and drink it? I was trying to do something *nice* for you." I felt my own face getting hot.

He stood up and pushed himself away from the table, the bottom of the chair squeaking against the linoleum floor. "*Thank you.* I don't want it!"

The microwave beeped with my finished hot chocolate. I balled my fingers up, my nails digging into my palms.

"Get out, Will," I said, my voice an angry-quiet I hoped my parents couldn't hear from the living room.

For a second, I felt guilty at the look in his little-kid eyes, but I couldn't stop myself now, after I'd already started. Besides, he was being mean.

"You can't tell me what to do," he whined.

"Just go away!"

Will shrieked then, and Mom came bounding into the kitchen a second later.

"WHAT is going on in here?"

"All I did was ask for marshmallows and she started screaming at me!" The sound of tears welled in his voice, and he sniffled.

"That's not what happened!" I told Mom.

"Why can't you just help him out? For my sake? He's your little brother!" Mom babied him so much it was ridiculous.

"I was! I just told him we were out of the marsh-mallows he wanted, and then he said he didn't want it, and now he's just being mean, and I didn't *do* anything!"

"I heard you tell him to go away! Where is he supposed to go, exactly?"

"I don't care where he goes—just away from *me!*"

"Louisa," she said, "if you haven't noticed, your father is very upset right now. It would be nice if you could just take care of things a little bit. You're not a little kid anymore."

"I was TRYING to be nice! I was making him hot chocolate."

She started rubbing her temples with her fingers. "I don't know what to say anymore. You've just got to give me a break. It's too much, all of us stuck inside going stir-crazy. You two *can't* fight."

"But it wasn't me! You always take his side, just because he's little, but—"

"Stop," she said.

"I'm going to my room, and HE *better not* follow me."

"It's his room, too. If he wants to go in, we're not going to stop him."

"There's no way for me to get away from anyone in this house! Ever!"

"Oh, *I* know," she said, and the look in her eyes

banged against me like I'd fallen off tall monkey bars into a sandpit below.

Maybe she hadn't meant to say that out loud, because she started stammering something after me, but I was already stomping down the hallway to my bedroom and didn't want to hear.

~ↄ

My room wasn't much of an escape, I already knew. Mom and Dad had tried to divide the space so that Will and I each had a side, but it was too small for that, really. Instead, the foot of my bed touched the head of his, and most of our stuff was squeezed wherever we could fit it.

Before we'd been forced inside, I hadn't even minded it that much. Sometimes Will asked me questions before we both fell asleep, and it relaxed me having him close. I had a red lantern hanging over my bed that turned the whole room this warm, orangey pink when the overhead lights were off, and I had space to line up all my special things on my dresser: my jewelry box, where I kept my charm bracelet; a giraffe figurine Mom made me when I was a baby; a picture of

Nellie, Priya, and me; my speaker that let me sync up music from Dad's computer.

Tonight, though, it felt like I was trapped inside a tiny dungeon. I sat on my bed and stared up at my lantern.

I heard someone at the door and prayed it wasn't Will.

"I'm coming in, Lou."

Dad swung the door open and poked his head inside.

"May I?" he asked, his voice playful.

"Yeah, I guess."

He closed the door behind him, walked to Will's bed, and took a seat.

"You okay in here?"

I took a deep breath and exhaled really loud.

Dad raised an eyebrow. "I know little brothers can be annoying, and besides, we're all feeling a little trapped. It's really tough," he said.

"Uh-huh," I said. When he was done talking, I would explain that I was actually *trying* to be nice to Will and *he'd* started fighting with me.

"But this apartment is not big enough for two angry kids," Dad continued.

"But—" I said, ready to plead my case.

"Louisa, he's your brother. You've got to look out for each other. And sometimes it's really hard," Dad said, his voice shaky. "Brian's like my brother, you know, and right now, I'd give anything to be able to fight with him. Talk to him. Anything."

I stared at my hands in my lap. I could hear Dad breathing kind of heavy. I wanted to tell him how upset I was about Brian, but I didn't want to make it any worse.

"Okay. Lecture over," Dad said.

Will's bed creaked as Dad stood up. He walked over to me, and he smelled clean, like the mint soap he used. The crinkles of his leathery skin folded around his eyes as he smiled down at me. He ruffled my ponytail and then turned to leave.

"Dad?"

"Yeah?"

"Mom's really mad at me," I said.

"No. She's just frustrated," he said. "Do you think Will was really mad at you about us being out of the marshmallows he wanted?"

"Probably not."

"He was mad about the situation we're in right now. Right? Like we all kind of are?"

"Yeah. I guess."

"That's the same thing as what happened with Mom."

"But Mom is a grown-up."

"Ah, Lou," he said, and then he chuckled. "Grown-ups get fed up, too."

"So it's about other stuff," I said.

I stared at him, wondering if he was waiting for Mom to start acting the way she had before, the same way I was.

Dad just nodded and turned toward the door.

"I really *was* trying to be nice to Will," I said.

"I know. I'm sure Mom knows that, too. Sometimes people take things out on the wrong person. Even adults. Try not to think about it anymore," he said.

After he was gone, I threw my head down on my pillow and turned to look out my window. The dark sky and the white moon formed this blue-gray blanket over the snowy backyard. I wished it were water so I could dive in and swim away.

Six

"*What episode of* The Marina *are you on?*"

Nellie was FaceTiming Priya and me from her fluffy white cloud of a bed, fuzzy silver pillows and a pink throw blanket wrapped around her. It looked a lot like Rhiannon's bedroom on *The Marina*, which was probably not a coincidence.

We'd just finished another remote meeting of Makers Club, and we'd set a FaceTime date for right after. It was sort of like how before the Freeze, we'd walk halfway home together after club meetings before going in our separate directions.

"I just watched the one where Alistair gets lost at sea on his sailboat right before midterms," I said.

"Ah! And the part when Jessie rescues him?"

"Oh. No, I didn't see that."

"It was a two-part episode! How could you not watch the second part?" Priya asked.

"I—um, well, Will wanted the TV," I said.

The truth was I didn't really care all that much about what happened to Alistair or his sailboat. I only watched it so I'd have something to talk to Nellie and Priya about.

"Well, you have to watch tonight and let me know when you finish," Nellie said.

"I will," I said. There was a lull in our conversation then, and I felt awkward, wondering why I couldn't think of anything else to say to them.

"Well, what *have* you been doing, if you're not watching *The Marina*?" Priya said after a few more seconds of silence.

I considered telling them about Brian's accident, how it loomed over our apartment like a rain cloud, and how sometimes I tried to put myself in his brain, wondering what its blankness felt like.

A week had passed since I'd visited Luke and he'd seemed so confident that Brian would be able to piece his memory back together. In the two weeks since the accident, my parents discussed Brian's recovery constantly, but I hadn't heard one hopeful update to support Luke's *Rodrigo*-inspired theory.

I decided not to tell Nellie and Priya any of this, though. I knew they didn't like Luke much.

Instead, I said, "I don't know. It's boring here. Every day's the same. What about you two?" I shifted on top of the itchy floral comforter Mom bought on sale at T.J.Maxx right before the Freeze started.

Priya shrugged, like she was agreeing with me.

"Something *is* new with me," Nellie said. "Adele's having a baby." Adele was her stepmom, who lived in Switzerland with Nellie's dad.

"What? Whoa!"

"That's so exciting!" Priya said.

Nellie fussed with the sleeve of her sweater. "Yeah," she said. "In Switzerland."

"Yeah," Priya said. "But you'll still see her. Right?"

"Yeah, if you count FaceTime," Nellie said. "But it doesn't really matter, because, you know, I might be moving to Switzerland."

"What?" I asked, not believing my ears.

"My mom said next month, if the snow isn't gone

by then. This is a really unsafe environment for kids to be around, with all the ice and snow. She said it's not good for me, and that she doesn't want it to have a negative impact on me," Nellie said.

I wondered why my parents thought this environment was fine for me, if it wasn't safe for Nellie.

"There's snow in Switzerland, too. This is global," Priya said.

"Well, Mom says Switzerland is more equipped to handle snow, and that it'll be better for me."

"How are you gonna fly there? I don't think moving when you don't have to is essential travel," Priya said.

Since the Freeze had gotten bad, most flights were grounded. The wings of planes were always freezing over, and the airport runways were coated in ice. Only essential air travel was permitted. Travelers needed to be granted approval on a case-by-case basis, and there were only a few flights every week.

"Because he's my dad, and I'm a minor, it could be considered essential. They're looking into it," Nellie said.

"My dad would never want me to leave right now. But you don't see your mom now anyway," Priya said.

Before the Freeze started, Nellie's mom had flown to Korea to be with Nellie's uncle, who was sick. Then, after the travel restrictions were put in place, she hadn't been able to fly back. Nellie's grandma, who she called Halmeoni, was staying with her and her older sister, Sonya, until their mom got back.

"I see my mom. We video chat," Nellie said. She blinked a few times in a row.

"Well, it'll be nice to be near the baby," I said.

"If you even end up going," Priya added.

"I *am* going. And I'm going to go to school in Europe. And I'm going to learn German and French."

This had to be way cooler than going to school here. Priya seemed to think so, too, because neither of us said anything else about it.

"What did you think of Mr. Rojas's assignment?" I asked, changing the subject.

During this week's Makers Club call, we'd gone over everyone's biggest challenges from the Freeze, and then we'd made a big list of the things people missed most about their lives before it. Our job for the next week was to brainstorm ways we could bring back what we missed most in our lives, even if the Freeze continued. That was why I'd left Nana off the list. I couldn't bring her back.

Priya cleared her throat. She looked bored, the way she had when I'd presented my current events article.

"What?" I asked.

"I don't know... I just... It seems stupid. I mean... we can't solve problems the Freeze caused. Don't you think if we could, adults would have fixed things already? I'm getting sick of Makers Club, anyway. Seriously, Mr. Rojas can be super annoying, starting these intense debates all the time," Priya said.

"Plus, it's mostly fifth graders," Nellie said.

The intense debates Mr. Rojas started were one of the things I liked most about the club. He made me feel like I could do important things, even though I was still a kid.

"It's *half* fifth grade and the rest of us are sixth," I said. "Maybe you just don't like having these video meetings. Maybe when we're back to school you'll like it again."

"Maybe," Nellie said, but she sounded unconvinced.

I looked down at my lap and studied my bitten fingernails.

Priya asked Nellie a question about their homework for Mr. Keller then, and my thoughts faded to my own math worksheet, still sitting untouched in the printer tray from that morning. Before we ended our call, Nellie reminded me to catch up on *The Marina*, and I promised I would.

Just so we'd have something to talk about.

～

The next afternoon, I sat at Luke's dining room table, watching him fly through word problems while I doodled on my math worksheet.

Mom and Alesha sat at the other end of the table, sipping tea out of hand-painted mugs. Alesha had lots of pretty, delicate trinkets around the apartment— some of them she brought back from her trips home to Jamaica, and others from flea market shopping.

I watched her twirl the tag of her teabag with her long fingers. "The other night, I stepped out in the backyard when I got home from the hospital and I looked out at all the snow, and it was so beautiful in the moonlight, and I just listened. I could finally hear myself think. It helped me come up with a plan for things."

I wondered what her plan was, but I noticed her eyes darting over toward Luke then. I got the feeling she wanted to talk to Mom about it without Luke hearing. I hated when adults did that.

"Can we take a break?" I said.

"Huh?" Luke lifted his head from his paper and stared blankly at me.

"I don't want to do this anymore," I said, pointing to my messy, doodled paper.

"Sure. I'm just checking these over anyway," he said, shrugging.

"I don't know why you'd spend one more minute than you have to with these problem sets," I said as I followed him into the living room.

I plopped down beside him on their comfy gray couch. Will welcomed us by picking up one of Luke's Rodrigo action figures and shoving it toward him. "Look!"

"That's Orion—he comes in book two. He can illuminate the sky," Luke said, and Will blinked in confusion.

"So, can he fly?" Will said.

Luke shook his head, joining Will on the rug. "He orbits, because he's composed of celestial materials. Orbiting isn't really the same as flying. When my dad gets better and he's home again, he's going to help me build a model—Orion's going to hover over the top of the moon with a string. When I build it, you'll see what I mean."

"When's your dad coming home?" Will asked. I was pretty sure Will didn't know how bad things were.

"*Will*—" I said, embarrassed, but Luke didn't miss a beat.

"Any day now."

"Really?" I said, wondering why Mom and Dad hadn't told me this news.

"Yep. He'll be home really soon," Luke said, but he looked a little worried.

I wondered if every time Luke thought of memory-less Brian, he got the same terrified feeling in his gut as I did.

~⦿

"So, Brian's coming home this week?"

I was setting the dinner table, and I peeked

over at Mom. She rinsed a piece of fish in the sink. "What? No."

"But Luke said he'd be home really soon," I said.

Mom dropped the fish into a pan on the counter with a splat. "Louisa—just...can you go see if Will finished his homework for me?"

I was annoyed. Mom expected me to be mature enough to help her with Will, and understand that she was stressed and sad, but I wasn't mature enough for her to fill me in about Brian.

Still, I did what she asked. Will had finished writing five sentences using his spelling words for the week. He was always complaining about homework, even when he barely had any.

When I walked back to the kitchen to let Mom know, she was staring out the window, facing away from me. She was on the phone with Dad—I could tell from the tone of her voice. "I'm sorry. Alesha just told me. No, not that he couldn't—he *wouldn't* try. They thought it would help him start to connect things. He started yelling at the doctor, and he shoved the guitar away. That's what Alesha said."

I stepped back from the doorway so that Mom wouldn't see me.

"The look in his eyes—she said he was like a stranger. What if he can't play anymore? What if that's it?"

I felt like I'd heard something that wasn't meant for me.

I skulked into the living room. It didn't make any sense. Brian had rejected the one thing that could point him in the right direction, to who he'd been before the accident—back to Luke, to Alesha, to Dad—his guitar. I couldn't figure out why he'd do that—but then, I guessed he wasn't the Brian I knew.

That night, I was sleepless. I got up and stared out my bedroom window at the yard below. It looked so pretty outside, the bright moon painting the snow gray-blue. I thought of Alesha then, standing outside, peaceful, finally feeling like she could hear herself think.

When my electronic clock read 11:30 PM, I opened my door really quietly, so that I wouldn't wake Will, and shut it behind me. As I crept down the hallway, I saw that the door to Mom and Dad's room was closed. Dad was working the night shift, and Mom was asleep—when she was awake she left it open.

She'd never even know if I went outside.

I stepped into my snow boots sitting by the door and pulled my coat on. When I slipped through our heavy front door, I turned the bolt behind me so that it wouldn't shut and I could get back in without a key.

The hallway felt different at night—everything was quiet, and the overhead light was dim. Even just one step outside our apartment, things seemed a little better.

A surge of excitement pulsed through me. I could go anywhere. Do anything.

Except not really, because the streets were covered in ice, and I was a sixth grader with no money.

The light flickered. Upstairs, a door slammed.

I could be kidnapped, having let myself out of the apartment in the middle of the night. Or, even worse, Mr. Khan, who lived in the apartment across from ours, might see me and tell my parents.

But I didn't want to go back inside.

Home had always been somewhere I wanted to be. Before the Freeze, at school, I couldn't wait to go home. I didn't even like sleepovers at other people's houses— I always missed my bed. It was strange to think about that now, when all I wanted was an escape.

I padded down the stairs. The door to the yard behind our building had a big window; I peered out.

The backyard was long and deep. Before all the snow, there'd been a patio, a patch of dirt where Alesha and Mom grew vegetables, and a bench along the shed. Now none of that was visible—fresh snow blanketed the ground like vanilla frosting on cake.

As I twisted the doorknob and stepped outside, the cold cut across my face—right away I felt winter collect around me.

In my rush to get outside, I'd forgotten my hat, scarf, and gloves. I felt the cold spark through me, like the electric shock you get from rubbing your socks on carpet. I rolled my hands up inside the long arms of my parka.

It was eerily quiet. All I heard was the whooshing of the wind as it passed me. My whole life I'd been surrounded by city sounds: traffic, beeping car horns, ambulances, fire trucks, music blaring from passing car stereos. It was the same backyard I'd always had, but it was different now; I felt like my whole world had changed and I was the only thing that had stayed the same.

Above me, stars shined white against the dark sky. The light from the moon illuminated the walls of snow and ice Brian and Dad had piled against the fence months ago. The walls were as tall as grown men.

Alesha was right—in the calm of the night, I felt clearheaded. No Will whining; no stale heat surging through the pipes around me; none of the heaviness that surrounded Mom and Dad.

I just wished it weren't *so* cold. Then I could stay out here longer, for hours even. I could finally have an escape from our tiny apartment, where everyone's feelings hung thick in the air.

There was plenty of snow in our yard. I could use it to build a structure big enough for me. Besides, for our Marvelous Metropolis project, all the buildings would have to be made of ice—we'd have to figure out a solution to keep warm. I could try it out myself.

I grabbed a thick branch off the ground—where our patio used to be—and began to sketch the outline of my house in the snow. I pictured how it would look, where it would sit. Then I drew the outline of the entrance, wide enough for two of me, and a big rectangle in the center of the yard, which would be the middle of the house. I moved quickly, shivering from the cold that bit at my skin even through my parka.

Slam.

I jumped, turning toward the sound.

The back door swung open and then shut again.

I sighed—it was just the wind; I must not have closed the door behind me all the way.

I lumbered through the snow as fast as I could to make sure the door hadn't locked behind me. When it opened fine, I returned to drawing my blueprint in the snow.

"Louisa?"

I jumped again and scanned the yard. Of course it was empty.

I looked up at our building—no one was standing in the windows, calling out. I must have imagined the voice—I was good at psyching myself out when I was anxious.

I turned back to the site of my ice-house-to-be.

"Over here!"

There was a flash of light. Luke was sitting beside his open bedroom window, staring at me. He'd turned the lamp on beside him.

As I trudged toward his window, icy wind stung my cheeks. I jumped up on the snow-covered recycling bin under his window; our parents used to yell at us for trying to climb on top of it when we were little.

"What're you doing out there?" Luke asked once I was sitting up on the bin, the cold of the metal lid slicing through my leggings.

"Nothing. Why are you awake?"

I was panting a little. I watched my misty dragon breath twirling in front of me, and I wondered if Luke would tell Alesha I was outside. I knew she'd tell Mom.

"I can't sleep," he said. "And you're not doing *nothing*."

I thought of Mom on the phone with Dad earlier, the terrible image of Brian rejecting his guitar—if I were Luke, I wouldn't be able to sleep, either.

Luke was expecting an explanation from me, I could see from the look in his eyes. I stared down at the top of the bin, shivers traveling up my spine. I couldn't stay outside much longer.

"How'd you know I was here?" I asked.

"I heard the back door slam."

"Oh. Right. Well, it's just me," I said, trying to sound casual.

"Yeah, but what are you doing?"

"Nothing."

"It looked like you were drawing something in the snow."

"No."

"You aren't going to tell me," he said, frustrated.

"All right, all right. Fine. I want to build something out here in the yard with all the snow. Like, a little house."

"Like that article that you shared for your current event with the architects and engineers making buildings out of snow?"

"Right."

"I wanna help," he said.

"Thanks," I said, "but it's just going to be for me."

"Well, it's my backyard, too."

This was true. Technically, we all shared the backyard. But out of all the apartments in our building, we were the only kids. All the other people were older, except for Ama, Mr. and Mrs. Owusu's baby, who we heard cry sometimes but rarely saw now. No other tenants had used the backyard for years.

But the house wouldn't be all mine if Luke helped. We'd have to share it, and I *already* had to share everything with Will.

"I don't even have my own room, Luke. I just want one place that's mine."

He nodded, but I could tell he was disappointed from the way his gaze lingered on the yard behind me.

"Will's not bad, really," Luke said.

"He really is," I said, and Luke gave me a little smile, but the heaviness in his eyes made me sad.

Guilt pooled up inside me; Mom's voice on the phone to Dad, the hopeful way Luke told Will that Brian would be home soon, the emptiness of their apartment without Brian. I could see Luke wanting an escape, too.

"Look, you can help. If you promise you won't tell anyone."

"I promise," he said, beaming.

"Meet me out here tomorrow. After we log off school?"

"Okay."

"Okay."

I gave him a little wave before I climbed down from the bin.

"Louisa?" he called after me.

"Yeah?"

"You should really get inside. Quick."

"I will. I promise."

Seven

The following afternoon, Luke sat on the floor of my bedroom.

It was April 1, and I'd banned Will from the room after he'd barraged me with April Fools' pranks all morning. Wasn't the fact that it was the beginning of April and the entire world was blanketed in snow enough of a prank?

Now, every few minutes, he'd knock on the door and run away. Luke was entertained by this—I was not.

"Maybe we could shape the house like a spacecraft."

I stared at Luke. His other suggestions included shaping our house like a star, a castle, and a crater. After a while, I realized that every idea he had was somehow related to *Rodrigo*. I was starting to think that including him had been a terrible mistake. This wasn't going to be some make-believe structure.

"I was thinking something else," I said.

"Oh. Okay. What?"

Luke had an eager look in his eyes as I stood up and grabbed a book off the bookshelf.

This past Christmas, before Nana died, she'd given me a book called *Our House: A History of Homes*. It was a heavy book with the title printed in gold foil on the cover, embossed so I could trace it with my fingers.

The table of contents was illustrated, and different house styles were listed on a timeline. It started way back, covering the first homes—caves—and it went up to the present day. I'd looked at the book a lot since Nana gave it to me—I liked to rank my favorite types of houses.

Luke's eyes were fixed on the book as I sat back down. "Whoa. That looks awesome."

I handed it to him and watched the reverent way

he slid his fingers across the cover. When he opened to the first page, his eyes caught the handwriting at the top, squished next to the title. I'd forgotten: Nana had written me a message.

> To my lovely Louisa, I hope this book inspires you on your journey to build great things. The houses in this book are beautiful, and I am sure that one day you will make something just as special. But remember, it's the people you love that make a house a home. Love, Nana

Luke read it quickly. "From your nana?"

I nodded. "It's not even for kids. It's for real architects."

"She was so cool. She always took things you cared about really seriously," he said.

I was touched that he'd noticed that about her. Of course, he knew her, but he'd never spent a ton of time with her.

As he flipped through the pages, we were both silent. After he'd inspected the book carefully, he closed it and stared at me, like he was about to ask me something important.

"What's your favorite type of house?" he asked.

"Oh. Well…to live in? Probably I'd live in a Queen Anne house, somewhere near a coast, on a cliff. But I really like Craftsman homes, too."

"Do you think we could build either of those?" he asked.

"Uh. Probably not," I said, giggling at the outrageous image of the two of us somehow creating a front porch of ice, building windows with wide shutters.

"I think we'll just need to focus on having it be big enough for us both, and also make sure it will be strong and will last. As long as it's a real house, I'll be happy," I said.

"LUKE!" Will screamed then, before slamming both his palms on the door. We heard him scurrying away.

"Can I go chase him?" Luke asked.

"Fine," I said, shrugging, and Luke smiled before sprinting out of my bedroom and after Will.

❧

The next afternoon, we began to build.

I'd bundled up in extra layers: a thermal under-shirt, a long-sleeve shirt, a cardigan, and my warm-est sweatshirt. My puffy white coat had barely closed over all of it. Every time I moved my arms they squeaked like rubber against the sides of my parka. I felt like a balloon threatening to pop.

Luke was already outside as I struggled across the yard to reach him. I was carrying two clear storage boxes, one in each hand, and the wind blew so strong against me I had to stop walking. I closed my eyes, waiting for it to pass.

Over the howling of the wind, I could hear Luke laughing. By the time I reached him, my eyes were tearing up. I dropped the storage boxes in front of me.

I'd done more research into how the Inuit build their igloos. They always start by packing snow into hard blocks. Then they use those blocks to create their structures. They also suggest building into slop-ing snow so you need fewer bricks to complete the structure. The right side of the yard had more snow piled up higher, like a mini mountain. Will had sled-ded down the slope only a few weeks ago.

We would build the house into the slope.

Our hardest snow was packed into walls along the fence, so we headed over to them with our containers. We'd fill them with the hard snow to create the blocks.

"Ready?" I asked.

"Ready."

We dug into the walls with our gloved hands and pulled the snow down, collecting it in the containers.

Neither of us said anything for a little while. Our soundtrack was the crushing of tightly packed snow, almost like the crunch of a thousand potato chips.

I knelt down, and with my thick-gloved hands I kneaded the mound of snow tight into the sides of the container.

I looked over at Luke, who was also on his knees now, trying to sculpt his ice pile into a sort of foundation for the base of our house.

I pulled more snow down off the wall and packed it inside the container.

"Have you been visiting your dad at the hospital?"

"Yeah," Luke said. "He doesn't remember anything yet. They think he might still be able to play guitar, though. But he won't try."

I was relieved that Luke knew what I'd heard

Mom telling Dad—I didn't like the idea of keeping a secret from him.

"What do you talk about, when you visit?"

He shrugged. "I talk to him about homework, and sometimes I help him play memory card games, like he's a little kid." From the way he said this, I could tell he didn't want to talk about it anymore.

"Well. When you go again, you can tell him I said hi, if you want," I said.

Luke raised his head to look at me. "Thanks," he said. "I will."

~&

A little while later, the door to the yard swung open. "Hello, hello!" Alesha stood in the doorway, holding a thermos. She was wearing a green-and-blue patterned scarf around her neck and white earmuffs.

"I brought you two some tea. You've got to stay warm," she said, and she set the thermos on the ground beside the doorway. "What are you building?"

I opened my mouth to answer, but Luke beat me to it. "Nothing," he said.

She raised an eyebrow. "Fine. No moms allowed,

huh? Well, come in soon—don't need you two turning into icicles," she said.

Luke sighed after the door swung shut behind her. "I didn't want anyone to know."

"Your mom's cool, though."

He rolled his eyes. "No one else can come in, right? Even once it's done and our parents see it—it's just ours, okay?"

"Right," I said.

We worked until it got too dark. We collected our snow blocks in the center of the yard—getting our materials ready before we started building the house itself. By then, we were both shivering as we stood back and stared at the start of our creation: a collection of barely visible blocks of snow piled on top of one another.

"Luke—doesn't it kind of look like we didn't even do anything at all?" I asked through chattering teeth.

"No. I see it. Don't you? See, that's the back wall, and up there, that's the roof," he said, his breath leaving a cloud in the air in front of us as he pointed at nothing.

"If you say so," I said before we rushed to the door.

On my way upstairs to my apartment, I felt lighter, even with my ice-covered snow boots weighing me down.

I wondered if I'd felt like this my whole life until the Freeze had taken over, and if I was just remembering what it meant to be happy: to think about nothing except what I was doing; to worry about myself, and not Mom.

Eight

"*I better make* a few different dinners for Alesha for next week, once Brian's back," Mom said, setting her coffee mug on the end table with a bang.

I jumped. It was the commercial break of *Wake Up, America.* I was lost in thought, debating asking Mom to buy me a snow camera with a special lens for capturing pictures of snowflakes.

"Next week?" I asked.

"She'll be busy worrying about him, making sure he's settled," Mom went on. "Of course, they'll send a visiting nurse in to check on him, and an occupational therapist, but she'll still be mostly on her own."

"What? He's coming home next *week*?"

"Luke didn't say anything to you?" Her head tilted with confusion, or maybe interest. "I saw you two playing outside yesterday, like the old days."

I bristled at her spying on us from the kitchen window, describing what she saw as *playing*. In the five days since we'd started building, we'd worked away every afternoon until it got dark, only taking breaks to warm up in the entryway when it got too cold.

"He said Brian wouldn't try playing the guitar, and that he still doesn't remember anything. He didn't say anything about Brian coming home," I said.

"Alesha only told him yesterday. Maybe it's hard for him to talk about," Mom said knowingly.

"But if he's coming home, that's good. Isn't it?"

"He's able to walk and talk. He can read and write. He's able to do all the tasks that they worried about when he first got hurt," she said.

"So, his memory *is* coming back a little, at least?"

"No."

"Well, then why are they sending him home?" I asked.

"He's getting stronger and healthier. Everything is moving in the right direction," she said.

"But they have to keep trying. If he's not remembering, he's not ready to come back," I said.

Mom reached for my hand across the couch. "You know, there's a chance that his memory won't come back," she said.

"A chance?"

She stared at our fingers braided together. "We can keep hoping that it does," she said.

"So, that's it? They're just going to send him home, even though his brain is still messed up and he doesn't know who he is or who his family is?"

Luke thought Brian was piecing his memories back together like Rodrigo, that he'd return once he could see the pathway home. Mom was making it sound like he'd only drift further and further away into the unknown.

"He's lucky to be alive," she said.

There was a thick lump in my throat when I swallowed. Lucky? I didn't agree. I went into my room then, leaving Mom to meal-prep for Alesha. Cooking wasn't going to fix Brian. Maybe nothing could.

In my room, I held the piece of *Teardrop* I'd stuck in the back of my bedside table drawer. I traced the cool, curved shape with my index finger and thought about Brian.

A lot of the time when I complained about something to Dad, he'd say, *Hey, Lou, who ever told you life was going to be fair?*

He never sounded angry when he said it, which always made me mad. Life *should* be fair, and I didn't like that he could just accept that it wasn't.

I had a feeling now that this was what he'd been telling me: Unfair things happened every day. Sometimes they'd happen to me.

I'd thought that the unfair thing that happened to me was Nana dying without a warning, without me getting to say goodbye, without me knowing the last time I was ever going to see her.

But now there was Brian.

Brian was a part of us, too. Holidays, birthdays, random Sunday dinners: He was always there, laughing in a wild way that made me laugh, too, even when I didn't know what was so funny. His booming singing voice was intertwined with my memories of summer vacations, packing up the Jeep and driving for hours, blasting songs by old men with guitars singing about the past and the country and love.

I didn't have space inside me to take this unfair thing that had happened to Brian and carry it around with me, too.

~ৎ

Not long after I'd gone to my room, I heard a voice at my door.

"Louisa?"

"Come in," I said, sitting up and shoving *Teardrop* into the back pocket of my jeans.

Luke leaned against the doorframe, bundled up in his green coat and snow boots for building.

"You can come closer, you know," I said.

He took a step inside.

"What are you doing here?" I asked.

"We have to go out and build. We've gotta finish the house."

"I know...it's just..."

He wouldn't meet my eyes. "You know my dad's coming home."

"Yeah. My mom just told me," I said.

"He still doesn't remember anything," he said,

twisting his black hat in his hands. His face was blotchy. "We've got to finish our house before he comes home."

"Okay...," I said. "I guess you'll be really busy when he gets back."

"No, it's...," Luke started, then mumbled, "I— I just can't be stuck in my apartment with him like this."

I wanted to tell him how sorry I felt for him and for Brian, but I wasn't sure how to say it, or if it would upset him, so I didn't.

I swallowed hard, jumped out of bed, and pulled on an extra sweater from my closet. "I have an idea. But we're gonna have to go find Mr. Yu," I said.

"Why?"

"We need the keys to the shed," I said, reaching for my scarf. "We'll need to get the big shovels from in there."

"We can't ask Mr. Yu. He'll want to know what we need. He'll ask too many questions. Besides, my dad always says I'm not allowed in the shed alone," Luke said.

Brian helped Mr. Yu, our landlord, with chores

around the building a lot during the day since Brian's gigs were usually at night. He organized the rakes and shovels Mr. Yu stored in the back shed, mowed the lawn in the summer, and helped keep track of Mr. Yu's running list of to-dos.

"He won't know," I said. "We'll put the shovels back."

"Louisa," Luke said. "My dad has everything in a very particular order. Next time he goes in, he'll notice things are different, and he'll get upset."

Luke was lying to himself. I understood this, because I lied to myself, too.

The Nana lie: that saying goodbye to her wouldn't have made a difference to me. The Mom lie: that she'd start acting the way she had before. The Dad lie: that nothing bad would ever happen to him on the job, because it wasn't really *that* dangerous.

I felt less alone, knowing that Luke lied to himself, too.

"We'll put them back when we're done. He'll never find out. It's our little secret, right?" I said, grabbing my pink-and-orange knit hat from the pile of dirty clothes at the foot of my bed.

Luke considered this for a second. "My dad has a copy of the key. I know where he keeps it," he said.

"Let's go," I said, pulling my hat down over my knotted hair.

~⁓

I followed Luke downstairs to his apartment and into his parents' bedroom. The last time I'd been inside it was when we were little, playing hide-and-seek.

Luke bolted to the small table tucked between the window and the bed and opened the drawer with a creak.

I stepped closer to the wooden dresser beside the door. A picture sat at the end of the dresser in a shiny gold frame—I could recognize Alesha right away, even as a kid. Irie, Alesha's mom, was hugging her tight, and they were sitting in the sand on the beach. It looked like they'd been caught in a laughing fit.

Luke had Alesha's eyes, big and brown, and he had her eyelashes, too. They curled perfectly, like little smiles.

"Is this in Jamaica?" I said, holding the frame up.

Luke was busy searching the drawer, the sound of

random objects colliding. He turned his head. "Yes," he said, distracted.

"There's really snow there, too? Like here?"

I tried to picture the tropical palm trees in the back of Alesha's photo covered in heavy snow, but it didn't fit.

"It's everywhere. Even Jamaica," he said, like this was obvious. "I can't find the keys! I know he leaves them in here. I don't think he would've moved them."

"You want help?"

"No," he said.

I sat with my legs crisscrossed on the rug. Opposite their bed, they had shelves that stretched from the ceiling to the floor: Brian's record collection, so many men with long hair on covers. There must have been hundreds of albums. Had Brian known all the songs? Could he play them all on his guitar? What was filling that place in his brain now?

Sometimes when we had dinner together, Brian and Dad would pick an album and play it on the record player and talk about every single song. It took hours and was always very boring, but now I wondered if it would ever happen again.

I tried to think of the last time this had happened, but Luke interrupted with the triumphant shake of a key chain.

"Let's go," he said, bolting to the door.

I jumped up and chased after him, even though I wanted to stay a little longer with my memories of Brian. I could see the lonely records waiting for him. But it felt like they belonged to a Brian that wasn't coming home.

Nine

After we'd taken the shovels, our work sped up, our countdown to Brian's return propelling us faster.

We'd begun placing our snow blocks in a circle—each block touched the one next to it. Then we started stacking our snow blocks on top of one another until they were almost taller than me. The shovels helped us pack extra snow around the edges of the blocks so that there were no gaps between them and the walls were thick.

Luke wanted us to build all afternoon every day, as soon as our remote school day ended. When Mom insisted I stay inside to watch Will while she did the laundry that Wednesday, I was sort of glad to have an excuse to give my arms a rest.

Will had been quiet as he'd played on his tablet—not an educational coding game, the way Mom had told him to, but some racing game. I'd let him get away with it, because it kept him busy, but now he was staring up at me, slamming his feet against the floor, that thumping again.

"I'm bored," he said.

"So?"

"So, I'm just super bored! Why can't we go outside?"

I reminded myself that he was only six. It was hard for him to be stuck inside, especially because he was the kind of kid who loved to run around and climb on things he wasn't supposed to climb on.

He plopped down next to me on the couch, his shaggy hair falling in front of his eyes, and started poking my arm again and again. "LOU. I'M BORED."

I slapped his hand away. He ignored me, tugging at my sleeve.

"I can't do anything about that!" I said, my eyes fixed on Dad's laptop screen. I was trying to read an article about first responders that Ms. Lee had assigned us for homework.

"Can we please, *please* go outside?"

"You have to ask Mom when she comes back," I said.

"It's not fair that you and Luke always get to play outside and I'm not even allowed to come," he said. "I wanna build with you."

He whined about this almost every time I bundled up to meet Luke. I always ignored it, along with the pleading looks from Mom or Dad. I deserved one place that I could escape to that didn't involve Will.

"Let's see what Mom says about going outside when she comes back."

He groaned, dropping my arm and burrowing into his side of the couch.

When the front door squeaked open a little while later, Mom lugging her laundry bag behind her, Will leapt up from the couch. "MOMMY! LOU'S GONNA TAKE ME OUTSIDE!"

"I didn't say that!" I said, putting Dad's laptop down on the rug in front of me.

Mom plopped the overflowing laundry bag on the floor and pulled her hair out of its elastic so that it dropped from its messy bun. "Louisa's not in charge of whether or not you can go outside."

Will hung his head low and his cheeks flushed

pink—this was the first step in a full-blown Will tantrum. She looked from him to me. "Why don't we *all* go out in the yard?" she said.

Mom hadn't played outside in the snow with us in months; she rarely even left our apartment.

Will bolted over to Mom and wrapped his arms around her tight. "Yes, Lou! We're going out!"

"Really?"

"Why not?" Mom said, giving me a pleasant shrug.

I was surprised by how happy I felt at the idea of doing something *fun* with her again.

~⁀◟

It was already dusk when we got outside. The wind was stronger than Will's little body; he fought against it to get to the middle of the yard.

Mom rubbed her hands together and bounced from foot to foot as she scanned the yard. "Your fort looks nice, Lou," she said, pointing to the ice house.

It was clearly still under construction. It kind of looked like a huge sideways melting bar of soap. "It's not done," I said.

"I still like it," she said. "I like where you're going with it. Very cool."

I dug my boots deep into the snow.

"What should we do?" Will asked.

I stared at him. "What do *you* want to do?"

"I dunno," he said, shrugging.

"Will, you wanted to come out here," Mom started, but then it seemed like she felt bad about not having a good idea, either. "Why don't we build something?" she suggested.

"Okay," Will said.

Mom wandered to inspect the snow farther away, and I felt silly for thinking she might play with us. Will started making ice shavings, like the snow cones we got on the boardwalk on summer trips to the beach.

"Hey, Lou," Mom called.

As soon as I turned to look at her, a snowball curved through the air, angled right for me, and exploded against my chest. "Hey!" I shouted.

Her laugh carried over the whistle of the wind.

Will was doubled over, his giggles contagious.

"How'd you even do that?" I called to her.

"Fresh packing snow over here. Come look."

Will and I shuffled our way over to Mom. I grabbed Will's hand as we walked. It felt like the wind might pick him up off his feet and fly him away.

We watched her roll the snow and ice, packing it together in a ball. "You have to make sure it's not too icy. Otherwise you could hurt someone."

She handed Will the half-formed snowball she held in her gloves and let him add a bit more snow. Then she stepped back and waved at him, like she was waiting for him to hit her.

His mouth hung open. I could actually *see* him thinking. He jumped up and down in excitement and then, with a twirl of his arms, propelled the snowball at Mom.

It was a good one, and Mom screamed very dramatically when it hit her.

I grabbed a handful of the snow. I rolled it just like Mom had, packing it tighter and tighter. Then I launched the snowball straight at Will's back. It collided against his blue parka, a *whack* cracking through the wind, and he shrieked.

"You okay?" I called out.

"You got me," he said, holding his hand to his heart. Then he started laughing and threw himself on the ground. He was actually being kind of funny.

I lay down next to him in the snow and stared up at the swampy-gray sky. Soon that navy-blue blanket of night would appear, telling us it was time to head inside.

I heard the crunching of Mom's heavy boots against the snow, her steps coming closer and then stopping.

She lay down beside Will.

"You two are so silly," she said. I could practically hear her smile.

"This is the best day ever," Will said.

I didn't correct him. I inhaled the smell of fresh snow and settled my eyes on the sliver of moon coming into focus.

~

Luke and I continued building the next afternoon.

The walls were standing up now, the blocks forming our circular house—it felt like a huge victory. Now we just had to make sure they'd be strong enough to support our ceiling.

"My dad was playing one of your dad's albums last night," I said.

We were taking extra snow and smearing it into the cracks like paste to make sure the blocks were all held together.

Luke peered up from behind the back wall of the house, which was taller than him now. "Really?"

"Yeah. The one with the old phone on the cover? I have one of the songs in my head now," I said.

"Which one?"

"I don't know the name. It goes like: *dun-dun— dee dum. Dee dum dun-dun.*"

Luke started laughing right in my face.

"None of his songs go like that."

"This one does!"

"What're the words?"

"Something about flowers...flowers in a dead garden? Something like that?" I said.

I liked Brian's music, but it always confused me— the tunes were happy but the words were sad.

"Sing it," Luke said.

The idea of singing a song aloud for him seemed super awkward, but I could tell from the eager look in his eyes how happy talking about Brian's music made him. I took a deep breath and started to sing, my voice shaky and off-key.

"Um, *dun dun dun...I saw the flowers in the garden, and they...*"

I was going to tell him I forgot the rest of the

words—I could feel my cheeks flushing, even in the freezing cold—but I heard him a second later.

"*They reminded me of you, and I'll never forget the way the petals wilted when winter came,*" he sang, his voice a little squeaky.

Singing together, our voices meeting in between the whooshes of wind, felt kind of silly, but it also felt familiar. I wondered if it made him think the same thing I was thinking: When we were eight years old, driving out to camp with our families, we sang on the way, "to make the time pass more quickly," according to Mom. I didn't remember anything else about the drive, except the sounds of Dad and Brian leading us through old favorites. They said it was our *musical education.* I would recognize the songs now, but I wouldn't know the names, so maybe it didn't totally work.

As we sang, I didn't feel embarrassed about my off-key voice, or about not knowing the right words. It was different from how I felt with Nellie and Priya when they started singing songs by Maude B, their favorite singer, and I hummed along, unsure of the lyrics—pretending.

We kept singing as we built that afternoon. Sometimes one of us would suggest a song, or one of us would hum and the other would join in.

Once we'd made sure our walls were thick enough, Luke and I crawled through the makeshift doorway.

Just then, I heard this scattering noise, like the sound of beads hitting a hardwood floor. I looked up, and something fell from the sky, a prickle of ice against my forehead.

"Hail!" Luke called, just as I wiped my forehead with the end of my scarf.

I grabbed my shovel and Luke grabbed his, and we both sprinted to the back door.

Standing in the foyer, I unwrapped my scarf while Luke peeled off his floppy hat. The overpowering building heat seeped into my eyes and nose and skin so that I felt itchy instantly. I rubbed my eyes as Luke slumped against the hallway wall.

He shook his head from side to side, and water splattered from his drenched hair onto me.

"Hey!"

"Sorry!" He bit his lip, but it didn't hide his laughter. "Think we'll finish before my dad comes home?"

"Yep," I said. If I agreed, I'd have to figure out a way to make it happen.

"Good."

"Are you...happy...he's coming home?"

"Yeah. Obviously," Luke said.

"Of course," I said.

His eyes fell to his feet. His wet boots and mine were creating one puddle, which was spreading across the floor.

"He'll start to remember more when he's home and around us all day every day," Luke said. He sounded sure. I couldn't tell if he actually believed it or if he was just really good at lying to himself.

"Know what would be cool?" I said, eager to stop wondering if Luke was about to have his heart broken.

"What?"

"If you could decide what memories he kept. Like, if you did something bad, you could make it so he wouldn't get that memory back," I said.

He looked at me. "Like the time you and I put that soup can in the microwave?"

"And my dad had to put the fire out?" I said.

"Or the time we brought those roly-poly bugs in from the backyard in that shoebox and they all got lost in his closet?"

"Yeah. Like that," I said.

"It would be better if I could get my mom to forget those things. My dad, he never gets that mad, really," Luke said.

"Yeah. He's always chill about things."

"But if he never remembers when we took that music award thingy and scratched our names in the back with that screwdriver? That would be fine," he said.

I snickered, remembering one of the few times I'd ever seen Brian get truly angry. He'd apologized later for yelling, taking us on a walk to get ice cream and talking to us about the importance of respecting other people's property.

Joking with Luke seemed to make us both feel a little better, but I couldn't help but wonder: If Brian really didn't remember things—even the bad things—would he still be Brian?

Ten

It was even colder than usual the day before Brian came home.

It was Friday, and Luke and I were racing against nightfall to complete the ice house.

The night before, we'd finished building our roof. Luke had stood on top of the slope of snow we'd built into, packing the layers on top of the blocks to complete our dome. I'd stood inside the house, checking to make sure everything was secure and there were no gaps from the inside—but ready to bolt out at the earliest sign of crumbling. Luckily, it was strong, and our roof (and Luke) didn't cave in on me.

Today I was wearing Dad's ski mask—I wouldn't

be stopped by a freezing nose or icy cheeks—but in it, I couldn't see to the right or left of me. Black fabric pooled at the sides of my eyes. I could hear Luke even though I couldn't see him: boots crunching against the snow, shovel scraping along the edges of the house to smooth it out.

When we'd started today, the opening to the house had been all jagged. It was wide enough for Luke and me to enter, but it was ugly, rough and unprofessional-looking. I thought of *Our House* and the idea of form versus function. Form was how something looked; function was how it worked. The function of our house was good, but the form was bad.

So I'd set out to improve the form.

With the backs of my ski gloves, I molded the snowy barrier along the entrance into a curve so that the doorway was round, the edges smooth. I clasped my hands around fresh snowballs and pushed them tightly along the edges of the opening, trying to create the look of a stone archway, like in one of the English Garden houses from the book.

I had to press hard and hold my hands against the snowy English Garden stones while I counted to one hundred. I felt shifting snow particles resisting the pressure as I pushed, connecting the snow-stones with the house.

When the arch looked close enough to what I had in my mind—except that some of the snow-stones I created were more rectangular than circular, and the ends were kind of falling apart—I stood up and dusted the ice off my ski pants.

The last thing we'd do after every building session was search for indents and holes and pack them with snow to make sure the structure was solid. This time, I spotted no holes as I circled the house, not even small ones.

Luke met me by the entrance as a pale blue blanket of sky tucked itself around the house. It was past dusk, and we were running out of light.

It wasn't what I'd imagined. Some of the blocks were uneven, so the right side of the house jutted out in front of the left, and the roof dipped low, a slope we hadn't planned. But the house sat there like an eager friend, almost like it'd been waiting for me all along.

I took a deep breath and stepped forward. My

knees hit the ice underneath me with a thud and I crawled through the entrance.

It was warm inside. Luke scooted against the far wall, and I moved next to him, my left knee touching his right.

We sat still together.

Through the walls, dark seemed to seep in, turning the house a purple-gray. I wasn't sure what to say, or do, afraid that the majesty of what we'd built would crack, fragile like glass.

Finally, I said, "Wow."

"Yeah," Luke whispered. "It's like we're on a different planet."

I let the mystery of it surround us while I imagined a world of ice buildings, a city made of ice schools and ice hospitals and ice palaces.

There was something shimmery about the walls—they sparkled a little, like they were made of finely crushed crystals.

"Finally," Luke said. His voice sounded louder than usual; maybe it echoed.

"Wait," I said, and I reached into the pocket of my parka and took out the glass piece of *Teardrop*.

I stood and walked to the entryway arch, pressing the smooth glass into the top of it.

"What do you think?" I said, taking a step back and admiring the shiny blue-green piece pressed against the ice.

"I love it," he said, then after a pause, "What is it?"

"A piece of one of my mom's old sculptures."

"It broke?"

I didn't want to relive the whole *Teardrop* drama, so I just nodded. "But I like that I have this piece— and it's kind of like a little piece of art in here."

I sat back down beside Luke, and we both stared up at it. Against the shimmering snow, it seemed to glow.

I turned to Luke. "So, what should we do?"

"*What*, are you *bored*?" Luke asked.

I thought about what Brian and Dad would always tell us when we complained about being bored during parties where it was all about the adults: *Get yourself un-bored*.

"I'm not bored," I said.

I put my head back and lay down on the ice, my hood the only thing protecting my hair from growing icicles.

The ceiling seemed to shimmer as I stared at it.

I thought about asking Luke if he noticed the sparkling, too, but I didn't want to jinx it. It felt like being inside a planetarium, exploring a strange new galaxy—but for some reason, I felt very safe, like I belonged to this unknown sky.

Eleven

The day Brian came home from the hospital, Luke spent the morning hiding out inside the ice house without me. I knew this because when I first woke up, I looked out my bedroom window and saw fresh footprints leading to the entrance.

A few minutes later, I stood outside the house in all my layers, blinking away the morning sun. It reflected off all the white snow. The glare made it hard to see.

"Luke?"

"Wait!" he called urgently.

I knelt down next to the doorway. "Why?"

"Just wait!"

I wondered if something terrible had happened, like maybe the house had started to collapse inside, but it looked fine from the outside.

When he poked his head through the doorway, his eyes were lit up in amazement.

"Something crazy happened," he said, out of breath.

"What?"

"Come," he said, returning inside.

I didn't love that Luke had a secret of his own about *our* ice house, but I brushed this off and followed him.

The floor of the house was packed with soft snow. Luke sprawled out on it, moving his arms and legs back and forth like he was making a snow angel.

"What are you doing?"

"Just do what I'm doing, and look up at the ceiling."

Instead, I watched him push the snow left and right with his arms and legs, tiny particles of snow dust billowing underneath him. His eyes were fixed on the ceiling—it didn't even seem like he was blinking.

I lay down beside him. My hair fanned out underneath me and mixed with the powdery snow.

"Now look up."

I did as instructed, getting lost in the shimmering snow of our roof.

"You see the sparkles, too," I whispered. It hadn't just been me. They'd been real.

"No. Make a snow angel. Just like I showed you."

"Why?"

"Just do it."

I waved my snow angel arms and legs, and I waited some more.

Finally, I said, "What's supposed to be happening?"

I could tell my question annoyed him. "Just wait," he said. "Don't think of anything at all, and keep doing what I'm doing. Keep your eyes up there."

An awful possibility crossed my mind then that this might be some Rodrigo-related thing, something I didn't get. Not a prank, exactly, because Luke wasn't into pranks. An extended game of make-believe, maybe. I could see Luke doing something like that.

I slid my arms and legs back and forth in the snow. I thought of snow angels. I thought of real angels. I thought of a little glass angel figurine Mom had made me a year or two ago, and wondered where I'd put it.

While my mind wandered to angels and glass figurines, it happened.

First, it was faint. I blinked five times in a row. I
thought my eyes were tired. I thought I was seeing
things.

The particles of snow—fine, dusty—seemed to
paint an image: my face, older, flickered in front of me.

"It's a mirror?"

"No," Luke said.

I kept staring, mesmerized at the impossibility of
it. It was like a murky, translucent image. Not quite
clear enough.

I stopped making my snow angel and watched
the image dissolve—each inch of my face, hair, eyes,
replaced with the emptiness of dusty snow.

"It's gone."

I was afraid to look at Luke in case something I'd
do would make it go away forever.

"Just keep moving," he whispered back.

He was kicking snow up onto me with his feet
frantically, like he, too, was afraid of what might happen if he stopped.

As soon as I moved my arms again, the image of
me was back.

I studied her, this me who was different. She was slightly out of focus, blurred in a way that improved me. Her light hair was longer, with gentle waves. A face more defined where mine was soft, and her skin looked healthy, almost glowy—not pasty, the way it was now. This Louisa looked right at me with piercing blue eyes: It was like she could see me as clearly as I could see her.

Something about the look in her eyes, the sense that she knew me, was terrifying. I stopped then and took slow, steady breaths to calm down: I was panting like I'd just run a marathon.

Beside me, Luke's eyes were still glued to the ceiling.

"What is this?" I asked him, shaking him by the shoulder.

"Stop!" he shouted.

"What?"

"Don't—I don't want it to stop," he said.

I noticed, looking closer, that his eyes were wet.

"Luke, what is this?"

He let out a very disappointed sigh and rolled over onto his side so we were face to face.

"Why'd you do that?" he asked.

"What's happening?"

"I have no idea what it is. Did you see something?"

"Yeah! I saw myself."

"That's it?"

"Well, myself, sort of. But almost...sort of, like, dreamy?"

He laughed then, which surprised me. "Dreamy? You were dreamy?"

I rolled my eyes. "I don't mean it like that, but like a dream. Not a picture, sort of different." I shook my head, like I was trying to wake myself up. "Luke, how did you just start seeing things?"

"I was lying on the snow, just stretching out, and I guess I was moving a little. I don't know. Anyway, yeah, it just happened."

"And what did you see?"

"Same as you."

"So, you saw *me*?"

"No, *me*," he said.

"How is it happening?"

"I have no idea," he said.

"Maybe something happened to us?" I said.

"Like what?"

"Frostbite, maybe?" I said.

On the news there were reports about people getting frostbite every other day, sometimes losing their thumbs or toes, getting to the hospital too late. Maybe this was a *form* of frostbite, a type that only affected the brain? It could be really serious.

"Luke, maybe we should get out of here."

He was staring at the ceiling, and I could tell he was about to start making another snow angel. "Why?"

I bit my chapped lip. "I'm scared."

He looked at me. "This is *our* house. There's nothing to be scared of here. Besides, I really don't want to go back inside."

"You can always come to my apartment, you know," I said, rubbing my hands together really fast until they felt hot. "We can wait for your dad together."

"We built this for times like . . . like when we don't want to be home," he said. He turned his head back to the ceiling.

This had to be some sort of trick of the imagination. Maybe it was like the dots I saw when I pressed my eyes too hard against my pillow at night.

"Just a few more minutes," I said.

As I followed his motions once more, the vision reappeared, and I felt this calmness, like falling asleep.

~⁓

Luke had to go inside eventually, when Alesha called him in to get ready for Brian's arrival. I stayed in our apartment with Will while Mom and Dad went to help Alesha and Luke bring Brian home.

Later that afternoon, I heard a door slam downstairs that echoed through my ears like a drum. I wanted to look, but I was afraid of what I'd see. I opened our heavy front door and stood on the landing, peering down into the hallway beneath me.

Dad was guiding Brian into his apartment by the arm, and my breath hitched in my throat. From where I stood, Brian looked pretty much the same as he always had. Mom was in the entryway, holding the door open for them. Alesha was behind Dad, who was looking at Brian with such sadness that I bolted back inside.

"What does he look like? Frankenstein?" Will said, staring at me from his spot on the couch.

"Don't say that. Brian could never be like Frankenstein."

"How do you know?"

"Because I know," I said—except I didn't know anything about this new Brian. He was a stranger—for all I knew I was lying to Will.

"He looks the same," I said, but Will was already back to his tablet.

E.T. was on TV. I'd seen it before because Dad loved it. It was an old movie about this alien that kids catch and keep in their house. He gets stranded on Earth, but he doesn't really belong. The kids keep him a secret. They love him, but he can't stay. For the first time I noticed how depressing it was. It was like I'd never understood it before.

When my parents came back upstairs that night, I pretended to be asleep on the couch. Dad draped a blanket over me and kissed me on the head. I heard Mom and him whispering in the kitchen, and I didn't even try to make out what they were saying. I didn't even want to know.

But there was something about the musty smell of old heat and the sound of them puttering around the kitchen, opening and closing cabinets, rattling knives and forks in their drawers, that comforted me.

Twelve

Someone was baking a cake.

Unfortunately, that someone was not in my apartment. The sweet smell of rising cake batter wafted into the living room through our heat vents.

I hoped it was Alesha baking, that Brian's first full day at home was going so well that she'd decided to celebrate. Maybe he'd started to remember, back in his own apartment, surrounded by his things.

On *The Marina*, Josie was begging her friend Rachel to forgive her for not defending her to their science teacher, Ms. Griffin, after she'd skipped a lab. I was only half watching—I wanted to tell Nellie I was catching up to her.

All the kids on this show had perfect lives with barely any real problems. I couldn't imagine them trading lives with me—they wouldn't last a week away from their towering, shiny boats and ice cream at the Sweet Shack.

Clap-clap!

"You're going back to school next week!"

"What?"

Mom clapped her hands together again.

"I just got an email from your school district. It says that due to the success of the city sanitation department's efforts to keep the streets clear and provide safe passage, schools will reopen next Monday."

"Next Monday?"

Mom squinted at her screen, checking the message again. "That's what it says."

I burrowed under the throw blanket tossed beside me on the couch.

"Isn't that good?" Mom asked, staring at me.

If she was waiting for me to jump up and down, she was going to be disappointed.

"It is," I said, pulling the blanket tighter around me.

Later, when Dad got home from work, a frigid draft of air followed him in from the hallway.

"Guess the heater works," Dad said, unraveling his green scarf. He stepped out of his huge boots, and Will lunged across the floor to grab his feet.

Dad took a few steps with Will hanging on to his ankles, moving real slow, like his muscles were sticks that could break in half any minute. Then he sat down next to me on the couch. He opened his arms wide like a stretching cat.

"*You* are a sight for sore eyes." Dad said this a lot; I didn't really know what it meant, but it made me feel good.

Will climbed up onto his lap.

"What did I miss?" Dad said.

Mom slinked over then, and she squeezed herself into the small space between Dad and me. Our family was too big for our couch.

I noticed Mom reaching for Dad's hand.

"Why does Daddy still have to go to work but you don't anymore?" Will said.

Mom dropped Dad's hand. "Well...what would you do all day if I were at the studio?" she said.

I hadn't thought of that. We'd be all alone when Dad was at work if Mom were still going to the studio every day. I'd be stuck taking care of Will all the time.

"I don't know. We'd go with you?" Will said.

She shook her head. "I want to be here, with you two."

"Dad," I said. "We're going back to school."

"You know something? I heard about that," he said, rubbing his hands along the back of his head so that his gray hair stood straight up.

"Happy?" he said. I shrugged. "It'll be okay," he said.

"I'm happy!" Will said.

Dad smiled at Will, but I got the feeling from the heavy look in his eyes that he felt more like me than like Will.

"Well, folks, that's another day down," Dad said after a minute.

When the Freeze first started, we'd counted the days we'd been stuck inside. We'd stopped counting days after weeks had passed, and we'd stopped counting weeks after months had passed.

"A gazillion more to go," I said.

"That's the spirit," Dad said as he ruffled my hair.

~⁀)

Remote learning was coming to an end, and Brian was back home, but nothing felt right. It seemed like the world was deciding we'd just have to get used to the Freeze, instead of stopping it altogether.

The next day, I signed in to our Morning Meeting with Ms. Lee in a huff. Things were changing, but not in a way that made me feel better. I'd gotten used to having my class video calls while sitting in the cozy window seat in my pajamas, taking breaks from my schoolwork to snack with my parents or Will, sneaking in some TV with Mom in between assignments.

"To all my terrific remote learners, a round of applause!" Ms. Lee said. She lifted her hands up to her camera and clapped them together, so that they were all we could see. Her nails were painted a shiny black, as always. When she was back in focus, she pushed her round silver glasses up on her nose a bit. "As I'm sure you've heard, I'll finally get to see all of you in person again, starting next Monday."

She paused, but I guess no one used the hand raise feature to say anything. I wondered if everyone else felt as confused about the prospect of returning to school as I did.

"To get us all excited, this morning I'm announcing our Sixth-Grade Spring Project! That way, you can start brainstorming before we're back together next week."

Every year, the sixth graders had a special project that they worked on for the last few months of school. It was a big deal—there was always a theme and a goal. Last year's theme had been *Under the Sea*, and the sixth graders had worked with local conservationists to reduce water pollution.

"This year, our theme is going to be *Living History*. I know what you're all thinking. . . . Do we really want to remember such a tough year? But we teachers were talking, and we started thinking about how you're going to think back to this once-in-a-lifetime event, the Freeze, and you'll want to remember what it was like for *you*. So we're going to be making a very special time capsule. We're going to incorporate symbols that represent your experience. And then, after we share them, you can all choose to take home your time capsule item and keep it somewhere safe to look at years from now."

Ms. Lee paused and grabbed a tall water bottle. I could hear her swallow over the microphone. "Any questions so far?"

No one said anything—everyone's faces looked blank. One kid, Enzo, was resting his head on his desk, possibly taking a nap. He wouldn't be able to do that again starting next week.

"Symbols are objects that represent something else—they stand for a feeling, or thought, or idea. You can write a song, or a story, or make art that incorporates symbols, and represents this year for you," Ms. Lee said. "Just remember, this isn't a *report* about the science being studied around the Freeze. This project is about using symbolism to represent personal, lived experience."

I'd thought going back to school would mean that the Freeze was over and we could finally forget it— this project seemed like we were commemorating it instead.

The *swoosh* of cresting waves joined the chorus of cawing seagulls as they flew overhead. I was in an orange sundress, chasing the water as it rose and fell along the shore, my skirt billowing out behind me.

Mom was chasing me. The sun beamed down on us. Our skin was sun-kissed. Mom's freckles imprinted darker along her cheeks and her bare arms.

I took a peek behind me. I was within her reach. I laughed, and she laughed, too, her smile blooming like a sunflower.

"Louisa. Louisa. *Lou-eee-sa!*"

I felt a tug on my arm. Mom, me, the beach: We all shattered into tiny particles of snow as I rolled over to face Luke. He was illuminated by the lantern-flashlight we kept between us so that we could come out here to the ice house after it got dark.

"What is it?"

His brown eyes pooled with guilt. "Sorry. It's just—my mom's calling for me."

"Huh?"

"We need to get out, or she'll come in looking for us."

I sat up straight. "I saw something different this time," I said.

"Me too." Luke secured his glasses on the bridge of his nose.

"My mom was there. We were at the beach." I could still see the flashes: the blue of her eyes, her flushed cheeks as she ran, the curve of her smile.

Luke was biting his lip. "I saw my dad."

"What was he doing?"

"He was playing guitar, singing. I was there, too. I was playing guitar with him."

"What song?"

"I didn't know it. Maybe one of his, but I'm not sure."

"You hadn't heard it before?"

He shook his head. "It wasn't a memory. Anyway, come on. Let's go."

I didn't want to leave, but I didn't want Alesha crawling inside our ice house, either.

"If it's not a memory, and it hasn't happened, what is it?" I asked once we were outside. The wind slammed against me like a wall of ice. It was dark out. The distant streetlamps from the sidewalk lit our way to the back door.

Luke didn't answer. I couldn't see his expression in the dark. He kicked the snow with the tip of his boot, the sound of scattering slush against dense snow breaking the silence.

"You think what we're seeing could really happen?" I asked.

Right then, the back door swung open. Alesha poked her head out, the hallway light flooding into the yard.

"Why do I have to come out here a second time?" Her voice sounded frayed.

I looked from Luke to Alesha, wondering if he was going to answer her, but the door slammed before he could.

He raised one of his bushy eyebrows. "I think my dad being home is getting to her," he said.

"Oh." I wondered if he'd get upset if I asked him more about having Brian home, but he'd sort of brought it up. "What's it like, having him back?"

He sighed. "I feel like he's not *really* back. It's like he's a stranger in my dad's body, sleeping in my dad's bed, living in my dad's skin."

"I thought maybe he'd remember everything as soon as he got back home. Or at least some things," I said.

We'd reached the door, and as we walked inside, Luke was silent. I wondered if I'd made him feel worse.

Finally, with a sigh, he said, "Me too. I know he will, though. I just need to figure out what will make it happen—what will make him play guitar again, the way I just saw him playing."

Trudging up the stairs to my apartment in my sopping-wet boots, I felt sure—what we'd seen in the ice house needed to be the future: if not for me and Mom, then for Luke and Brian.

Thirteen

The next afternoon, the blade of Mom's peeler clicked as she swiped at the wet skin of the potato in her hand.

I looked from her pile of potato skin shavings to mine. I wasn't doing this right. Chunks of potato the size of French fries were lying on the paper towel in front of me.

Dad had brought them home from the firehouse; one of his friends had gotten extra. Potatoes were hearty plants, but even they were getting more scarce. We'd mostly been eating food that Mom and Dad bought in bulk and froze for months, so this felt like sort of a big deal. Dad had been very proud of his potato haul, and Mom had promised to make cheesy mashed potatoes for us. We'd bring some down to Luke's apartment, too.

"Priya and Nellie must be excited to go back to school, huh? Get Makers Club back up and running in person?" Mom straightened the paper towel she was piling the skins on. "Be careful with your fingers there, on the edge of the blade," she added.

"Okay. I don't know about Makers Club, though. I... It's kind of..."

"I miss Nana's mashed potatoes. They were the best, weren't they?" Mom said, placing her perfectly peeled potatoes in a big orange bowl.

I swallowed my thoughts about Nellie, and Priya, and Makers Club. It didn't matter—the only thing Mom could focus on was her broken heart.

"They were my favorite in the whole world. I always told her that," I said. If the only thing Mom wanted was to miss Nana with me, I could do that.

The last time I'd gone to Nana's, she'd made us roast chicken and mashed potatoes with the skins lumped in, which sounded like it would be gross but was actually so good.

Thinking of that night made me feel guilty. I'd sat

at her dinner table, scarfing down the mashed potatoes, anxious to go home and call Nellie.

I couldn't even remember what Nana had talked
about. I only remembered that as usual, she smelled
like the lavender Crabtree & Evelyn lotion she kept
on her dresser, and that when she hugged me goodbye she'd slipped twenty dollars into the pocket of my
parka and said, "A little treat for you and Will," like
she sometimes did.

❧

Our living room was very bright the next morning,
which made me want to crawl back into bed. Instead,
I was sitting on the couch across from my parents, who
were staring at me like they had some really difficult
new chore for me.

"We just want to prepare you a little," Mom said,
running her palm up and down the leg of her jeans.

"Okay," I said.

Because I was keeping Luke company in our ice
house, I'd avoided seeing Brian in the three days since
he'd been home from the hospital, even though my
parents had taken turns visiting him every day.

But Mom and Dad had decided it was time. I got

this sick feeling thinking about what it would be like to face Brian. I didn't want to be a stranger to him.

"Brian may seem different to you. He might sound a little different, and act a little different. You have to remind yourself that he's still the Brian we love inside, even if he doesn't remember us right now," Dad said. Something in his voice made me wonder if he really believed this.

"Okay," I said, mostly because I knew I couldn't fight them. I was hit with a wave of sympathy for Luke—he didn't have a choice; he had to deal with this new Brian every day. He couldn't avoid Brian the way I had. "But what if he says something strange and Alesha or Luke gets upset?"

Mom turned to Dad, who said nothing. "Uh, if that happens, which it probably won't, you just... you wait," she said, her face a question mark.

"Wait for what?" I asked.

I saw something in her eyes, maybe fear, before she said, "Wait... for the moment to pass. Or... you can change the subject."

"It'll get easier," Dad lied.

I knew we'd probably get used to it, but it would always be very terrible, like what happened to Nana.

Mom was going to stay upstairs with Will; he didn't have to go see Brian, because he was little, and he could still be treated like a little kid. Not like me.

~∾

Dad and I walked downstairs together. When we got to Luke's front door, Dad rested his hand on my shoulder.

"God, Louisa, this is hard."

I'd never seen Dad look nervous before, not ever, and I suddenly wanted to run back upstairs and wrap my arms around Mom and never leave our apartment again. But before I could, Dad knocked on the door, and Alesha answered.

"Oh, Louisa. It's so good to see you. Luke, honey! Louisa is here. Brian's doing a lot better today. Being home has been so good for him. He's more comfortable, you know?"

Alesha seemed exactly the same as she had before Brian's accident—not tense like she'd been a few nights before, yelling at Luke for being outside so late. She ushered us inside, where everything smelled nice—she had a vanilla candle burning on the dining room table, and light was streaming in through the open window blinds.

"He's got to feel better, being home," Dad said.

"Louisa, come say hello to Brian. He'll love it," Alesha said, and I looked at Dad with desperate eyes.

"Well, maybe I should check in with him first— make sure he's up for company?" Dad said, and I felt relieved, but Alesha was already leading me into the bedroom.

All Brian's brainpower should have been focused on remembering Luke and Alesha, and maybe Dad— not saying hi to me—but no one asked me, so I followed Alesha and Dad to Brian's room.

Outside his bedroom door, I took a deep breath, and the air rattled around in my throat. I was terrified to see Brian; my conversation with Mom and Dad had actually made me more anxious.

I stood next to Dad at the foot of Brian's bed.

Brian was sitting up, wearing a flannel shirt, with a relaxed look on his face. For a minute, even though deep down I knew it couldn't be true, I thought everyone must be wrong. He *had* to remember us. He looked like Brian—just a sleepy, paler version.

But then I heard Alesha say, "Brian, Louisa is here to say hello. Louisa is Mike and Gracie's daughter."

She was using her calmest yoga voice, and I exhaled really loud, almost like a lion's breath. She rested her hand on my back, and I felt it shaking.

"Hi there, Louisa," Brian said. His words came out kind of slow, with extra spaces in between them, but for a minute I felt a jolt of excitement. It seemed like maybe he did remember me; my name in his voice sounded so familiar.

"Hi, Brian. We live upstairs," I said, because no one else was filling the empty spaces.

"Yes," he said, his voice pleasant and peaceful.

Dad said, "How you doing today, Bri?"

"Good. Good," Brian said, nodding.

"Yeah. It's been a good day, hasn't it?" Alesha said.

I studied Brian. His eyes were different.

"There's a lot of snow out there," Brian said, pointing to the window, and I thought of how boring it must be to sit and stare out at snow all day.

"Yeah, it's kind of a problem," Dad said, and he and Alesha chuckled a little, but of course it was actually a huge problem—it was the reason Brian had no more memory.

No one seemed to know what to say after that. Alesha got this worried look in her eyes; so did Dad.

"Okay, Louisa, why don't you go see Luke," Dad

said after an awkward silence, and I felt so relieved at the prospect of escaping this terrible room that I almost jumped.

I found Luke in the living room. He was rewatching an episode of *Rodrigo* I'd watched with him before, but I plopped down next to him on the couch anyway.

"How are things?" I asked.

When he looked at me, I could see behind the smudges on his glasses. His eyes looked stunned, like a camera had flashed too close to his face.

"Sometimes I kind of wish he was somewhere else," he said.

When Dad came out and said it was time to go back upstairs, I jumped off the couch and rushed after him.

It had felt like the right thing to do, visiting Luke, so I wasn't sure why if I'd done the right thing, I still felt so bad.

Fourteen

I began a thorough inspection of the roof of our ice house the next afternoon; I *had* to see if there was any physical explanation for our visions. Maybe there was some special sort of ice formation growing on the ceiling that had created a prism. It wouldn't explain why Luke's snow angel had started the visions, but maybe if there was *something* unexpected about the roof, we could start to make sense of the whole thing. I climbed up the massive slope of snow behind the house to get a good look at the top.

From above, our curved roof looked impressive. There were some cracks I hadn't known about—gaps we hadn't been able to fill from inside—but there was nothing unexpected-looking about it. My only discovery was that it wasn't soundproof. I could hear Luke knocking into the wall—I figured he was banging his knuckles against it as he made his snow angel.

"Nothing there," I said, once I was back inside the house.

Luke glanced at me. "Okay."

I scooted closer to him and unzipped my parka. I didn't need to be quite so bundled up in here.

"What is that?" I pointed to a large wooden shape mostly hiding behind Luke's leg.

"Don't laugh," he said, picking it up. Now I could see that it was one of Brian's old guitars.

"What are you doing with that?"

He mumbled something into the collar of his coat, eyes firmly set on his boots.

"What?"

"I'm gonna learn to play," he said, still into his collar but this time clearer.

"Cool," I said. "Are you learning for your dad?"

He held the guitar, resting it on his thigh, and rubbed the sloped wood on the side.

"If he won't play, I'll play for him."

I didn't say anything else about it, but at this thought I got a feeling like the satisfying snap of a cap on top of a marker.

"So, what do you think is really going on? What do you think we saw?" I asked.

Luke raised his eyebrows at me, plucking the guitar strings one after the other.

"It's not our imaginations, is it?"

"It's not," he said.

"Do—do you think it's *magic*?" I whispered.

The way the particles of shimmering ceiling ice shifted back and forth like sand to form a perfect image wasn't the abracadabra, spells, flashing lights kind of magic, obviously, but it was unexplainable.

"Well, I can't think of any scientific explanation," Luke said.

"Right. Magic's not real, though, Luke."

I saw excitement well in his eyes. "Maybe, you know, it's like one of those unexplained things that happens. Like, in Roswell, in New Mexico, people see aliens," he said.

"No they don't."

"They *do*, Louisa. It happens. But the people that

see the aliens know that if they say anything, no one will believe them. Maybe it's some kind of extraordinary *event*. Something similar could be happening to other kids all over the world, and we're part of the event, but no one believes kids, so no one is talking about it."

It was pretty cool to think about us being part of the same secret kept around the world—other kids like us seeing visions somewhere special to them during this wild, destructive freeze.

"But why us?" I asked. Maybe the universe had chosen us because of how sad things had been for us lately.

"What do you mean?"

"I mean, *why us*," I repeated, and then I waited, hoping he'd come up with the same theory as me.

"Probably as a reward," he said.

"A reward for what?"

"Well, because instead of just complaining about the snow, we made something amazing out of it," he said, plucking at his guitar strings.

"You think?"

"I do," he said.

"And what do you think it is that we're seeing? The future?"

He took his fingers off the strings, resting them on the body of the guitar.

"Maybe it shows us the thing that would make us happiest in the world," he said.

"What would the point of that be?" I asked.

"I don't know. Does there have to be a point? I think magic is good enough all by itself, without having a purpose," he said.

"Whatever. That's not it, anyway," I said.

"How do you know?"

"Because if it were just showing us the thing that we want most in the world coming true, I'd be seeing something different."

"Maybe what you're seeing *is* what would make you happier than anything else in the world, but you just don't know."

"I know," I said.

"How can you say that for sure?"

"Because if it were showing us the thing that would make us happiest, I'd see my nana alive again."

"Oh. And she wasn't there?" he asked, his voice trailing off.

"No."

"Oh," Luke said. "I'm sorry." His voice was sad—I knew he meant it.

"It's okay. But that's why it has to be the future, something that could actually happen."

"Well, what *is* special about what you're seeing?" Luke asked.

Seeing Mom in the sunlight, truly happy, made me believe that when the Freeze ended, my life would feel normal again, but there was something else, too. When I was watching her in the vision, I felt totally safe.

"I guess...I guess seeing my mom so...I don't know, so okay? So happy?" I said.

I tried to say this in a way that expressed something I wasn't really sure how to explain or talk about to anyone.

"Your mom isn't...okay now?"

"No, no, she is. But ever since my nana died, she's just...different. So seeing her happy, not stressed or sad—it reminds me of when things made more sense," I said.

"I get it," Luke said.

Of course he did. I was complaining about how Mom was acting different; Brian was kind of a completely different person now. Maybe this was why it was easier for me to talk to Luke about hard things than to Nellie or Priya.

"So for some reason, we're able to see the future," he said. "And probably, some other kids somewhere, they're getting to see their futures, too. Even if kids told their parents, I bet their parents wouldn't believe them. I bet a lot of adults, even if they could see it, like if they physically saw what we were seeing, they wouldn't believe it. They wouldn't let themselves believe it."

"Why not?"

"Because adults have to have an explanation for everything. And if they can't explain it, they'll just ignore it. Like your dad, he's always giving us updates from the fire chief, because he wants to give us an explanation."

"Right. Or like Ms. Lee with the Freeze. She keeps talking about different hypotheses and theories and tests and how things are going to be proven and blah, blah, blah, but really, she has no idea."

"Uh-huh. Instead of just saying *I'm not sure*, she gives explanations," he said.

"So, it's kind of like, instead of wasting time saying *Oh, we know how this is going to be fixed*, like Ms. Lee, we should just fix things ourselves," I said.

He squinted at me. "What things?"

"If we like what we're seeing in the ceiling, and we think it could be the future, we have to decide to make it come true," I said.

I dug my boots deeper into the icy snow packed tightly beneath us. I watched the cold air billow out of Luke's mouth like white smoke.

"Like you, learning guitar for your dad. We can figure out a way to fix my mom and help your dad get better." My voice was a whisper, and I twisted my mouth, watching him for an answer.

"Somehow," he said, his voice really low. "It'll be harder with us at school during the day now."

"We'll figure it out," I said.

Luke looked at me. "I don't want to go back," he mumbled.

"Me neither! My mom keeps telling me I'll be happier once I'm back. She said it's too *isolating* at home. But I don't know; I kind of just got used to this. Now, something else..."

"Yeah," Luke said. "But what about Nellie and

Priya? You were together all the time before. Don't you miss them?"

I noticed a curiosity in his eyes, and I felt awkward, thinking of the way they both treated him. Despite the fact that Luke sometimes could seem oblivious to things, I got the sense that he knew they made fun of him sometimes.

"Yep. I'll be happy to see them again," I said. After the words left my mouth, I felt like I'd lied, but I hadn't meant to. I bit my lip. "It feels kind of weird with them, though. We've spent so long apart now."

"Really?" he said, his eyes wide.

I was surprised that I was telling him this, but it felt better getting it off my chest. I couldn't talk to Mom about it; she was too overwhelmed with her own stuff.

"They aren't into Makers Club anymore, either. Only Maude B and *The Marina*."

"Ugh," Luke said, making a gagging face.

"It's not that bad," I said, and he looked mystified.

"Anyway, I'll join Makers Club," he said. "Obviously I have lots of experience making things now."

I pictured Luke sitting beside me with his doodle-covered binder—Rodrigo, stars and moons and cartoons all over the front and back. Wondering what Nellie and Priya would say about his sudden appearance at my side filled me with dread. Plus, I was the president of Makers Club—it was mine. I didn't know how I felt about Luke slipping in. I liked hanging out with him here, in our house, just the two of us, but the idea of him suddenly colliding with my school life? I couldn't see it working out.

I smiled, but inside I felt uneasy.

"We're still keeping this a secret, though, right?" I said, waving my hand toward the wall.

"Tell no one," he said, his voice very serious. I laughed, and his frown broke into a smile.

～૭

I tried to enjoy my last day of remote learning that Friday. I spent the whole day in my pajamas, and Will and I watched TV for a long time after our lunch break. But knowing that Monday I'd be back in school made me too anxious to really relax.

Sunday, I prepared myself as best as I could to go back to school: making sure I had my backpack and papers organized, cleaning up the books and games

I'd left out in my room, picking out a red sweater and jeans to wear.

But that night, I stared up at the unlit lantern above my bed, listening to Will's steady snoring, filled with dread.

I got out of bed and walked down the hallway to Mom and Dad's bedroom. Dad was at work. Mom's door was open a crack. I pushed it gently and saw Mom lying on her bed.

She turned toward the hallway light. "Come in," she said.

I climbed in next to her, pulled her heavy wool blanket up over us both, and snuggled close to her.

"Can't you sleep?" she asked.

"No."

"You nervous?"

"No," I lied.

"It'll be fine when you get there. Everyone's feeling the same way."

I didn't say anything, just tucked my head into the crook of her arm.

"You've been lonely here, Lou. You won't even realize how glad you are to get back to normal until you're there."

I rolled my eyes. We both knew life wouldn't be back to normal tomorrow, no matter what she said.

～♋

The cafeteria smelled like bleach. There were two janitors mopping up the puddles that collected as snow melted off all our boots.

The soaked furry insides of my heavy snow boots were now squishing around under my toes. I'd left my parka and hat on when I'd sat down at a bench in the cafeteria. All my extra layers—parka, sweater, thermal undershirt—made me feel like I should be outside, shoveling our front walk, not back in school.

Nellie sat across the table from me. Her black hair was pulled back in two buns on either side of her neck, and she was wearing a magenta faux-fur coat. If it started to snow on her walk home, I imagined the wet pink fur would get matted down like a dog caught in the rain.

"Halmeoni almost didn't let me come today," Nellie said.

"Really?"

"She thinks it's too early for us to be traveling," she said.

"My dad thinks it's fine," Priya said, her eyes fixed on the graphic novel she'd brought with her.

"Well, you know, she just really wants me to be safe."

Dad knew a lot about safety, and he seemed fine with Will and me returning to school. I didn't say this, though.

"*Everyone's* family wants them to be safe," Priya said.

"I know," Nellie said.

"Louisa's here, and her dad would know. Right?"

I gave them both a noncommittal smile.

"Besides," Priya said, still looking at her book, "I thought I was gonna go crazy if we didn't come back soon. Not that I want to be in class. Ugh. But just, like, I missed everyone, and my brother and my dad were driving me insane."

She looked at me then, something unsure in her eyes.

"Yeah," I said, "I get it," but I thought about how when we FaceTimed, Priya had always seemed like she was having fun at home, watching movies with her brother and getting quality time with her dad.

"Did Will drive you crazy?" she asked.

Before I could answer, I noticed Nellie's and Priya's eyes focused on someone behind me.

"Hi."

I turned around. Luke was standing there with this expectant look on his face, like I was going to greet him with a huge smile and invite him to sit down.

"Hey," I said. As I scooted over to make space for him I shot Nellie a glance, pretending I was annoyed. I hoped Luke didn't see it. Priya raised an eyebrow and looked from me to Luke. Then, turning to Nellie, she asked about Maude B's latest romance.

"My dad played some music last night," Luke said, apparently oblivious to Nellie and Priya.

"He did?" I said, grateful for the distraction.

"Yep. Tom Petty. He's always loved him. He listened to every song on his album, the way he used to, and he hummed along. He even knew some of the words."

"That's amazing! It's starting to happen already," I said, but before Luke could answer, I felt Nellie's eyes on me.

"What're you talking about?" Priya asked.

"Oh. Nothing. Any of you think of an idea for the time capsule project yet?" I said, drumming my fingers on the table.

"Not yet," Luke said.

"It's kind of a stupid project," Priya said. "No one wants to remember this."

We all murmured in agreement. I tried to ignore the looks Nellie kept shooting Priya—I knew she wanted Luke to leave. I hoped he didn't notice.

The cafeteria was filled with kids now. The janitors were mopping ferociously, and teachers were flooding into the room, lining the wall in preparation for the homeroom bell.

My palms were getting really sweaty. I stared at Luke, thinking of our house—I wished we were there, where things were easier.

∽୨

After school, when I was wrapped up in a blanket on our couch, it was easy to forget that today had been different from all the days before.

"So...Lou?" Mom said, peering over her laptop screen at me, her eyebrows raised. "How was it? Did it feel nice being back?"

"So cool!" Will said. The whole way home from school, he hadn't stopped talking about his friends, his teacher, choice time and indoor recess.

"She was asking *me*," I reminded him. He shrugged and grabbed a piece of popcorn from the bowl I'd made for us.

"It was okay," I said.

"Just okay?"

"Well, there was one thing," I said. I'd been thinking about how to ask Mom to help with my project all day. If she helped me to make a piece of symbolic art out of glass, I knew she'd feel better—more like her old self.

I glanced over at her. Her eyes were focused on her screen again. "Hmm?"

"Well, we talked about our time capsule project."

"Yeah?"

"I have to make something that symbolizes what this year has meant for me, and then we'll present it, then keep it to look at again one day when we're old."

"When you're old? How old?"

"I don't know...maybe like ten years from now? But anyway, I had an idea. I wanna make something out of glass with you. Like a figurine or a sculpture," I said.

Mom's mouth straightened into a thin line.

"It could even be really small." My voice was a little shaky.

Mom sighed. "You know I gave up my studio."

Mom hadn't actually confirmed this, not to me, so I'd let myself believe that she'd decided to keep the space a little longer.

"And second, even if that weren't the case, it wouldn't be your project if I did it for you."

"I'd help," I said. "You always said you'd teach me."

"Twelve is not old enough, first of all," she said, rubbing her eyes.

"Maybe I could draw what I wanted, like design it, and you could make it. It wouldn't even take a long time—it could be super small."

Mom stretched her arms up toward the ceiling. She closed her laptop. "No," she said.

"But why?"

"Louisa."

"Mom."

For a split second, I thought I saw a sliver of regret in her eyes. Then she stood up.

"I want you to come up with your own project, something totally yours."

"This *would* be mine. I just wanted to do it with you."

"Think of something else," she said, her voice sharp.

I lunged off the couch, bundled up in my parka, and stomped downstairs.

Outside, I lay on the floor of our house and watched a delighted version of Mom dance around in her bare feet, leaving footprints in the sand.

I liked Mom better in the future.

Fifteen

After school the next day, in the ice house, I told Luke that Mom had rejected my time capsule project idea.

"I thought if I reminded her how much she loved making her work with my project, she'd go back to it, and that would help her get over missing Nana. It'd give her something exciting to do, and then she'd start to get happy again, the way she looks in the ceiling," I said. "It could be like her version of your dad's guitar—the thing that could make everything click for her again, and make her feel like her old self."

Luke seemed to turn this idea over in his mind for a minute.

"Then this project's not the way—if it was, it would have worked," he said. His matter-of-fact tone annoyed me.

"How do you know that?"

"Well, think about it. In *Rodrigo*, sometimes he thinks he's interpreted a clue the right way, but then he realizes he hasn't. He's on a path that's not going to lead him anywhere—a dead end, almost. That's what this is. When you figure out what'll fix her, it'll work."

"*Okay*," I said, slightly annoyed that things had turned to Rodrigo once again, "but how am I supposed to figure that out?"

"It'll be obvious. An opportunity just hasn't come up yet," he said.

Luke looked silly on the floor of the ice house in his parka, playing guitar, his eyebrows wrinkling in concentration.

"What's the song you're learning?" I said, stretching my leg up in the air above me, my boot pressing against the curved wall of the house.

He continued strumming at his strings, ignoring me.

"Luke?"

He strummed off-key then, the sound angry, and

rested the guitar on the ground in front of him. He looked annoyed.

"I'm trying to play the song I saw in the ceiling. But I can't. I can't remember it, and I can't really play, anyway."

"Oh. Do you think it *is* one of your dad's old songs?"

"I don't know. There are a lot of them, I guess. It sounded like it could have been. But I didn't remember it."

"What if we play some of his old music? Maybe if we play his old albums, you'll recognize it? And then you can learn it?"

Luke's eyes lit up. "Louisa, you're a genius!"

I beamed. I could feel my cheeks bumping into my eyes.

He was already standing up and getting his stuff together.

"Where are you going?" I asked.

"I need to look for his old music."

"It won't be hard to find," I said. Sometimes Dad played us parts of Brian's old concerts on YouTube, and it always felt funny to see him in front of a huge crowd, spotlights shining down on him.

"No, there's some music that he recorded before. Like, it isn't well known. I don't know if he ever even released it. It's on CDs that he keeps in this black binder. If what I heard *is* one of his songs, it would have to be on that first CD. I know all his other ones."

"Would you ask your mom?" I said.

"Ask what?"

"To play you that album."

"No way. This is *our* secret, right?"

"Right," I said.

That Friday, we had our first in-person meeting of Makers Club since the start of the Freeze.

Mr. Rojas's classroom didn't look like the others in our school. Instead of corny inspirational posters or charts with math formulas, his walls were lined with intricate scientific diagrams: parts of plants, or illustrations of physics concepts like force and motion. They were neatly labeled, and Mr. Rojas encouraged us all to stand in front of them and observe them like you would in a museum.

He'd started the meeting off by reminding us that we had to decide our first steps to build our new

Marvelous Metropolis project by the end of the meeting if we were going to finish it in time to submit it to the judges.

During our remote meetings, he'd made a list of the biggest challenges the Freeze had created for us, as well as the things we missed most about life before the Freeze: traveling, swimming pools, the beach, soccer fields, basketball courts in the park, a field to run around in without getting wet, restaurants and stores, visiting family that lived far away, seeing friends easily, long walks, playing tag, not being cold all the time. He presented the list on the board now.

Instead of inspiring me to brainstorm solutions, seeing all these missing elements of my old life listed one after the other gave me a heavy, sinking feeling. I didn't want to focus on how to adapt to our *new* environment. Luke and I were busy trying to figure out how to get our old one back.

"So," Mr. Rojas said, "how are you going to fix this?"

It was silent. Across the table, Nellie was making a note in the corner of her notebook page, and Priya was reading it.

I'd been happy when they'd taken their seats

across from me at the start of the meeting, but I'd felt horrible when Nellie had rolled her eyes as Luke sat beside me.

Even though they'd shown up, the way they sat side by side whispering and passing notes made me feel like I wasn't a part of them anymore.

"Well, *we* really can't fix it," Keisha said.

"What do you mean?"

"These are things that adults should be working on and coming up with better solutions for," she said.

Mr. Rojas's eyes lit up. He was clearly excited about the debate her answer could spark. "And what if adults can't come up with the solutions? What do you do then?"

"How could we, if expert adults can't?" Andre asked.

"What if it *were* up to you to address these problems? What if you fifteen kids *are* the only ones who can solve these problems we've identified? What would you do?"

"I guess we'd come up with one idea and try it. Like, vote on one way to solve a problem as a group, and try it, and then change things if it doesn't work?" Luke said.

"Trial and error. Collaboration. Very nice," Mr. Rojas said.

"We could build a city out of ice that has a way for us to do everything on this list. We could at least try," I said.

Mr. Rojas moved to the SMART Board. He picked up a pen and in scrawling blue digital ink wrote: *Structures to Be Built (Out of Ice).*

"Start shouting out some ideas," he said, holding his pen at the ready.

"Sidewalks safe from ice and snow," I said, and as Mr. Rojas wrote down my words, I felt a flicker of excitement at the idea of solving a problem when so much seemed unsolvable.

∿

Luke showed up to the ice house late the next day. It was Saturday, and we'd planned to meet early—I'd scarfed down my breakfast. When Luke did arrive, he edged inside on his knees, his hat falling off, his sneakers untied. He carried something bulky in his arms. It looked sort of like the alarm clock radio my parents had in their room.

"Sorry," he said, his breathing heavy, "I had to

wait until my mom and my dad were both in the living room. Then I went through these big boxes my dad has in his closet with all his old music stuff. If he was his old self, he'd be so mad at me for digging through it.... It's off-limits."

"*And?*" I couldn't wait any longer.

"Yeah. I found this CD. It's labeled *One*. It's the first album he ever recorded," Luke said, plopping down on the ice beside me. "Never released it—it's a demo. I found his old CD player, too." He set it down on the ground in front of us.

"So now we just hope you can recognize it," I said, rubbing my hands together.

He took the CD out of its case and loaded it in the player. After he hit the play button, there was a whirring sound, like an engine revving, and then three loud clicks. I was afraid the CD was broken.

"Luke...," I said, but he held his hand up. A second later, I heard Brian's voice.

"*Wednesdays, wandering as the days slip by,*" he sang. His voice sounded higher than it did now, and a little creaky—less practiced, maybe?

The song seemed to be about a car, and how fast time

was moving. It was nothing like the music Brian sang now, but I liked it. Somehow it made me think of the stories Dad told about the two of them in high school, how they hung out in Brian's garage after classes, playing music and talking about moving to the city.

About halfway through the song, I tapped Luke's knee.

"Is this it?"

Luke shook his head. "I don't recognize it."

He pushed the forward button, and a second later, a different song began playing. The first minute was just guitar, and it was pretty boring.

Without a word, Luke skipped to the next song. He continued like this, listening to the first thirty seconds or so of each track, and then, with a shake of his head, skipping forward.

When he moved on to song six, which based on the CD case label was the last one, I held my breath and prayed he'd recognize it.

Lyin' awake, the door slammed behind you.
Summer gone. You were the last of the good
ones.

> *Those carefree days have faded to blue, the*
> *color I think of when I think of you.*

Luke perked up.

"This is it! This is the song he's singing on the ceiling!" He pressed the volume button so that the music blared through the speakers, and I straightened, focusing on the words and the rhythm.

> *If you showed up here now, at my door, even*
> *after all these days—*
> *I wouldn't think about the things that hurt*
> *me.*
> *I wouldn't think about the tears.*
> *I wouldn't think about the ten dollars I lent*
> *you,*
> *Just the ways you took away my fears.*

When the song ended, there was a crackling sound, and then Brian said, "That's it," and he laughed like a kid.

Luke pressed the stop button.

"That's the song?" I said.

"That's it. I recognized it right away."

"But you'd never heard it before? Your dad never sang it for you?"

"No. Never," he said, sounding a little mystified.

"You think you could learn to play it?"

He shrugged. "I don't know. I can try."

"So he was a teenager when he recorded that?" I asked, thinking of the framed photo of Brian in the bright pink shirt hanging in their hallway.

Luke nodded, a proud look in his eyes. "Sounded like he was a kid, kind of. Right?"

I nodded. "I think that might be my favorite song of his ever," I said, hitting the rewind button.

Luke didn't say anything else, but when the song began again, he started to shake his feet to the rhythm.

Sixteen

On *Monday,* I got to Ms. Lee's class late.

There was one seat left, and it was in between the window and Andre. As I settled in, putting my backpack beneath my chair and looking to see where Luke and Nellie and Priya were sitting, I noticed a buzz. The other kids had index cards on their desks. I saw Nellie in the front row, and she was leaning across the aisle to talk to Ignacio, holding her card in her hand.

The time capsule project. We were supposed to hand in a title and a description today.

I felt nauseous. As I scanned the room, I saw that *everyone* had at least one card sitting on their desk.

Andre looked at me. "You forgot?"

"Yeah," I said. I bit my lip.

"Sucks," he said, shaking his head.

"I don't know what to do."

"Go give Lee some sob story. She won't care," he said.

I didn't have any other choice. It would be worse if she found out later.

I felt woozy padding up to Ms. Lee's desk. The sneakers I'd changed into at school squeaked against the rubbery floors.

Ms. Lee seemed very focused on reading something on her laptop, and I took a deep breath. When I exhaled, I made this coughing sound that quickly got her attention.

"Are you okay?" she asked.

"No," I said, wringing my sweaty hands.

"Oh. What's going on?" she asked, her voice dropping lower.

"I can't do the assignment for the time capsule. I mean, I can, I guess, but I know we're supposed to have our idea already, and I don't have one. I mean, I *had* one, but it turns out I can't do it. I don't know what I could do instead. I know it's supposed to be a project to help us remember what this year was like, but I don't even want to remember it, really."

Ms. Lee pushed a piece of her shiny black hair behind her ear and sighed. "Louisa, it's okay," she said. "Honestly, you're not the only one who feels this way. Believe me." She never spoke this way with us—like a real person, not a teacher. "You know, the idea was really just supposed to be a creative way of capturing what your life is like right now. If things aren't great, it's okay to be honest. We can brainstorm together if you want, or you can have some more time."

She looked at me, concerned, and I felt my eyes water. I blinked a lot, hoping she wouldn't notice.

"I'll keep thinking," I said, relief washing over me.

As soon as I was back in my seat, Andre said, "Did it work? What'd you tell her?"

"Just the truth," I said.

He seemed less interested then, and as Ms. Lee stood up and turned the SMART Board on, my eyes trailed to the frost collecting on the window beside me.

~

Luke wasn't in the ice house when I looked for him after school that Wednesday, so I went back inside to find him.

Alesha led me to her bedroom, where Luke was sitting on the floor in front of Brian.

I paused in the doorway, feeling like an intruder.

"Say hi. Brian will love seeing you," Alesha said, and she ushered me in. Luke was slumped over like a bag of laundry, his chin resting on his fist. Right away, I could see he was miserable, but he gave me a halfhearted wave.

I walked toward him. Brian was staring at me. "Hi," I said. My voice sounded too loud.

"Hello!" Brian said.

"Brian, remember, you used to call Louisa *Louie*," Alesha said.

Of course Brian didn't remember. Luke shook his head beside me, like maybe he thought Alesha was being ridiculous.

"Louie," Brian repeated, something about his eyes making me feel like he was super focused, the way I'd be focused on memorizing a fact for a social studies quiz.

"Yeah," I said, "and you used to sing me funny songs on your guitar. Like made-up songs about my name."

He smiled, but I could see that he was frustrated, the sharpness in his eyes fading, almost glazing over the way Will's did when he daydreamed.

I pictured the inside of his brain as a factory with a mechanical gear turning, slow and careful, and imagined that he was trying to force it to go faster, pushing the pieces back together.

"Guitar," he said. "You know—I know... musician, you know? Your, uh, your dad."

Alesha was rubbing her palms together, and Luke was staring down at the gray patterned rug beneath us. I felt like I'd said the wrong thing.

"Yeah, my dad was in your band," I said, because no one else was saying anything. "In high school."

"Band," Brian repeated.

The longer I stared at him with my forced smile, the worse I felt. I couldn't imagine how frustrating this was for Luke.

I looked at the blank spot on the deep blue wall behind Brian, hoping he wouldn't notice that I couldn't look at *him* anymore.

"Why don't you and Luke go hang out," Alesha said after a few more painful seconds of silence.

"Okay," I said, still awkward-smiling, and followed Luke to the door. Before I left their room, I looked back at Alesha and Brian.

"Nice to see you, Brian," I said. This was a lie. Seeing Brian with his lost eyes and broken memory was not nice.

～૭

By the time I caught up with Luke, he'd thrown himself facedown on his bed.

"Luke?"

He rolled onto his side and sighed really loud. "Do you see how crazy things are here? He's—he's not... *him*."

I pulled my parka off and threw it on his desk chair, then leaned against the desk and bit my thumb cuticles.

"I don't know why my mom won't just admit it to me," he said.

"I hate when adults don't tell you what's really going on," I said.

I climbed onto his bed and leaned my head against his cool gray wall.

"Yeah. I just wish she'd tell me," he said, and I went back to biting my cuticles. I didn't think it would help him to be sure that his worst fear was coming true.

"I guess it's just—sometimes it's hard to believe he *really* doesn't remember. I heard my mom talking about me to him yesterday—and he said I *seem* like a very nice boy."

I felt myself wincing at the hurt in Luke's voice.

"And my mom has been trying to surround him with things so he'll remember, playing his favorite music, showing him family pictures, putting on reruns of the stupid old TV shows he likes. I just want to tell her to give up."

"She can't give up," I said. "You can't, either."

He shrugged.

"Luke—think about what you saw. You know he'll play again—you've seen it. She hasn't, so she doesn't know."

"I don't know, I've just been thinking so much about how I want to play for him, but then hearing his music—he's just a way better guitarist than I'll ever be."

"That's not true," I said. "He's had way more practice than you, Luke."

He looked like a sad, mopey puppy, and I wondered for the first time if encouraging him was wrong.

Seventeen

"Let's go with ice cubes as the primary building material," Luke said.

We'd begun building our Marvelous Metropolis model at Makers Club, but after we'd used sets of clear blocks to represent blocks of ice to set a foundation for our hospital, school, and apartment buildings, an argument about the best materials to use had broken out. It was hard for Luke and me to take other club members' ideas seriously when we were the only ones who'd built our own house out of ice.

"What about icicle beams?" Keisha asked.

"Like, long icicles? Maybe, but how would we make them strong enough?" I said.

"Maybe somehow we could engineer pillars out of icicles, I mean."

I wasn't sure about this, but I wanted to stop talking about what we were going to do and actually do it.

Nellie and Andre were working on creating a park with areas to play basketball and tennis and soccer. Nellie was using a stick and cling wrap to represent an awning that would keep snow off the soccer field. Priya was sitting next to her, a book open on her lap.

"Priya, you wanna work on the school with me?" I asked. She looked at me, her finger holding her place in the book.

"I'll just watch," she said. I wasn't the one who'd come up with this project, but for some reason I felt responsible for her boredom.

At the end of our meeting, after we'd cleaned up our materials and stowed the model safely on the counter in the back of Mr. Rojas's room, he had us sit down again.

He sat on his desk and looked at us.

"You know, this isn't my project. It's yours," he said. "My job is just to make sure that you have what you need to complete *your* vision. When I hear you debating the best way to solve a problem—what materials to use, how to build something—I get excited. It's important. One of the good things about the contest shifting and focusing on the Freeze is that it gives you an opportunity to think about how to solve problems that you're actually facing right now. It's your present, and your future. You're the ones who will live with this long after I'm gone."

I raised my hand. Mr. Rojas nodded at me.

"Do you think...that the Freeze is supposed to happen? Like, should we really accept it?" I said. "I think it'd be better to figure out ways to solve the Freeze, not the problems it's causing. So doing all of this, it seems kind of wrong."

Mr. Rojas looked at me, kindness in his eyes. "I wish I had an answer for you. But no one really knows for sure. So sometimes, when we can't solve the cause of something, it makes sense to try to fix its effects."

The careful look in his eyes gave me the feeling he was trying to pick the right words to comfort me. It didn't change the fact that I wished there were just *one* adult with a definitive explanation for me.

"This is ridiculous."

Luke's guitar strings made a terrible screeching sound as he strummed hard against them.

"What?"

"I can't do this. I don't get it. My dad made it look so easy."

I'd found Luke in our ice house, watching a video of a chord progression that was integral to Brian's song. Luke's fingers didn't move as quickly as the player in the video, and there was this awkward pause in between each pair of chords as he fumbled strumming.

He set the guitar down in front of him and hugged his legs to his chest.

"My dad wasn't *that* much older than me when he recorded that song, and he could play so well."

It was true—Brian had sounded really young. Listening to his first songs, I could easily picture him and Dad sitting on the front stoop of one of their houses, strumming their guitars and singing about girls they liked, or growing up, or moving on, or how confusing life could be.

"He'd been playing a long time, though. You've been playing for no time at all. It takes practice."

Luke nodded, a thoughtful look in his eyes. "Listening to his music from back then is kind of weird, isn't it?" he said.

"What do you mean?"

"He didn't know me then. He didn't know I was going to even exist. He wrote these words back then—so it's almost like I get to know a part of him from before."

"I like that," I said.

"He'll have to get to know me all over again, I guess," Luke mumbled.

"You don't know that. What if when he hears you playing his old song, his memories start to come back?" I said.

"Why would that happen?"

"Maybe hearing this song he wrote so long ago could help him remember what he felt like back then. It could connect him to his earlier memories, like when he wrote it—and then it could click. It's an idea," I said, and Luke seemed to consider this.

"You know, when your dad comes over, he plays for him sometimes," he said, staring down at his feet.

"Really?" I knew Dad visited every day, but a lot of the time he did this when I was in school, or out with Luke in the ice house.

"Yeah. He plays a lot of music that they liked in high school, I think. Sometimes my dad hums along. And once or twice I've come in and listened, and my dad gets this look—I guess it's weird, but—it seems like he looks more alive... like someone's inside... like he's not lost anymore."

"Like he's finding the pieces," I said, and then, "sort of like in *Rodrigo*?"

Luke's eyes lit up. "Yeah, it's just like that— like maybe your dad playing my dad's old favorite songs to him is helping him connect the pieces in his brain."

"And when you play his song for him, you'll be the missing piece," I said.

"Then everything will click, just like in book four: *Dream in the Dark*," said Luke.

I hadn't been forced to watch that episode yet, but I'd been the one who brought Rodrigo up this time, so I nodded enthusiastically.

~

As excited as I was for our plan, sitting on the ice while Luke learned to play guitar made me feel like an audience member, instead of his partner. He would bring his tablet out and watch YouTube video after YouTube video on learning chords, and rhythms, and strumming patterns. He would replay the same tune five or ten times in a row. If I could have learned to play by osmosis, I'd have been a seasoned guitarist by now.

But I couldn't. So I'd come up with a different idea.

When I went outside to meet Luke the next day, I carried a pair of bongo drums in my arms.

"I have a surprise for you," I said.

I sat down beside Luke, whose eyes were locked on the ceiling, his arms and legs flicking snow dust up and down.

"Luke," I said.

He stopped then and rolled over to look at me.

"Yes?" he said.

"Sorry, but... I have a surprise." I put the drums down in front of me and palmed the smooth tops with my hands.

His face softened. "Drums?" He pulled himself up. He picked up the bongos and turned them around, inspecting them. "Where'd you find them?"

"My parents left them on my bookshelf in my room. I don't know where they got them," I said, wondering for the first time *why* the drums had been left in my room without explanation.

"Well, it's a good thing they did," he said. "Now you can be a part of the song."

I was totally still, breathing in the crisp, snowy air between us. I felt my heart flashing like a firefly at the thought of being a *real* part of the thing that was going to fix Brian.

I didn't say a word. I just gave the drums a light palm.

The first song we tried together, Luke didn't sing any words. He just strummed his guitar strings. I tried really carefully to time when to hit. When he stopped strumming, I hit the drums really loud. It was an ugly, off-beat slam.

I was embarrassed, but Luke looked excited. "Isn't it fun?" he said. "Okay, let's try a different thing. I'll start."

He was trying to transition to another song with

a cool chord progression, which he'd been practicing for a while now. He wasn't good at it. Truthfully,
I wasn't sure he'd really even learned the chords
that well.

I felt this twistiness deep down as I watched him,
waiting for my moment to begin drumming, because
we were literally trying to make his dream come true.
I didn't want to think about what would happen if we
failed.

～�

*"The rise in unemployment has reached unprecedented
heights this week across the globe. This, along with the
reduced public transportation and limited supplies, has
inspired local communities to roll up their sleeves and
help one another out."*

Dad slammed his mug down on the coffee table
and turned off the news with a groan.

I was sitting next to him on the couch, my notebook opened to a blank page, a pen in my hand.

"Dad, can I ask you something?"

"Uh-huh," he said. I could tell he wasn't really paying attention.

"Well... I don't know what to do for my project. I need an idea."

"What project?" he asked, sitting up straighter.

"This time capsule project. I told you about it," I said.

He rubbed his hands over his face and then stared at me with red-rimmed eyes. "I thought you had an idea."

"I *did*. It's just that I wanted Mom to help me with it. And she said no."

"Why does Mom need to help you with it?"

"Because I wanted to make something out of glass, an art piece, a symbol of this year. And I wanted to do glassblowing. Mom always said I could do it with her when I was older, and I feel like I'm old enough now. Or at least I could have helped design it, and then she could have made it. I mean—she'd help me. But now..."

"You know that her glassblowing something you designed wouldn't be the same as you doing it, right? And, I mean, you're definitely not old enough to work with molten glass, Louisa. So she'd have to do it all."

I sighed, tossing my notebook down on the floor. "Do you ever just wanna fix something, Dad?" I asked.

Dad had a strong jaw, and when he was thinking about something really hard, like now, he'd push it out in front of his lips. "Uh-huh," he said.

He looked serious, and for a second I thought he was going to tell me something grown-up I didn't know, but all he did was nod.

"I wish I knew how to make things better," I said.

"What kind of things?" he asked.

"Well, the Freeze, I guess. But also, like, how people feel."

He gave me a knowing look. "*People*, huh?"

"I thought maybe if Mom helped me with my project, she'd remember that she used to be happy making things. She'd start to feel better."

He nodded. "Right. But it's not your job to fix anyone, you know. Not even Mom."

"But what if I want to fix things for her?" I asked.

He wrapped one of his arms around me. "Besides being nice, and good, and helpful—the way you already are—you're going to find out that it's actually pretty impossible to fix things for someone else. Even your mom."

I leaned against him, and after another minute he said, "Would it make you feel better if I helped you come up with an idea? With some art thing *we* could do together?"

I could see that he didn't really want to offer this. He wasn't the most artistic person.

"I don't know," I said.

Dad laughed really hard then. We both knew he couldn't help me, at least not if I wanted to do a good job.

"Hey," he said a minute later, "how's everything else going? How're Nellie and Priya?"

"I don't know. It's different," I said.

"It's been months without school. It's going to feel different," he said.

"But it's like *they're* different. I have to think of things to talk to them about. It's never been that way with them before."

"Maybe they're thinking the same thing about you right now," he said.

"You think I'm different than I was before the Freeze?"

Dad shrugged. "You seem a little wiser. All those gray hairs," he said, the corners of his eyes crinkling.

∽

A few minutes later, I trudged into the kitchen, where Mom was busy with something on her computer. She waved me over.

I stood beside her at her chair, and she wrapped an arm around me. I wondered if she could feel my heart beating fast—I could feel it in my throat. I didn't want to tell her that I still had no plan for my project, but this was a last resort.

"It's late, Lou. Think it's time you get ready for bed?"

"Well, I didn't finish my homework," I said.

"Why not?" Mom said. She stretched her neck like she was trying to get a crick out.

"I just couldn't think of another project idea."

"For your time capsule project? Louisa, you've had time."

"I know! I just... I only had my idea for us to work on together—it was the only thing I could think of."

"Well, I told you I couldn't help with that," she said, her voice heavy. She didn't say it, but I knew it made her sorry.

"But why not? Why can't you just do this one thing for me?" I asked.

"Louisa," she said, sounding tense, "I wish I didn't feel this way. But I just can't."

Sometimes, like now, I could look at Mom and know that her heart and her brain didn't match.

"I miss how you were before," I said. "I know Nana died, but *you* didn't."

"What?" she said, her mouth hanging open.

I didn't know what to say. I had a feeling I shouldn't have said this, even though I'd been thinking it for so long.

"I'm sorry you feel that way," she said, a startled, wounded look in her eyes.

Her being sorry wasn't going to fix it; I wondered if anything could.

Eighteen

We had recess in the gym every day.

All of the sixth grade crowded inside the sweaty room, most of us collecting on the rickety blue bleachers along the basketball court sidelines. If you didn't want to go to the gym, your only other option was the library, which was really drafty, and you weren't allowed to talk inside.

Nellie, Priya, and I were sitting on the bleachers, near the far basketball hoop. I stretched my legs out in front of me and pulled at the knee of my heart-print leggings, which had a snag.

"I think Maude B will have her first North American tour as soon as the Freeze ends, and we should get tickets," Priya said. Her hair was tucked into two French braids down the sides of her face, and she twirled the ends as she spoke.

"Sonya said she's gonna stream a secret concert on Instagram, but only for her true fans," Nellie said, her eyes glued to her phone. Sonya kept Nellie informed on all things social media. Nellie was holding her phone to her side so that Coach Amir wouldn't see; we weren't supposed to take our phones out at all during the school day.

"What do you think?" Priya asked, turning toward me.

"Yeah," I said, nodding like I understood what they were debating. "I think a secret concert," I said. I had no idea, but agreeing with Nellie seemed safe. I wasn't allowed to have an Instagram account and knew nothing about secret concerts—I'd never even been to a *regular* concert.

Nellie smirked, looking up from her phone to bask in being correct, but Priya just shrugged.

"I just don't get how she can tell who her *true* fans are, and only invite them," Priya said.

"Good point," I said.

The conversation petered out then. Nellie and

Priya both seemed annoyed, but I didn't know how to smooth things over. It used to be that I could just make a joke, and they'd both start laughing, and we'd move on. But now I couldn't come up with anything that we'd all think was funny.

I watched a group of kids scrambling for a basketball that rolled across the floor, the squeaking of their sneakers making me cringe.

"What's your time capsule project about, Priya?" I asked, once it was clear that neither Priya nor Nellie was going to initiate a new conversation.

Priya's eyes lit up. "Mine is really special," she said. "My uncle Rajiv lives in India, and my grandpa lives in Australia. They've both been sending me local stories and pictures of their yards covered in snow and ice, and I'm going to make a mixed-media collage of everything they've sent me and my own pictures of the Freeze here. In Australia, they had to wait for special shovels to be shipped in. It never snows in the part of Australia my grandpa lives in and it started in their spring! So they didn't have any supplies. Anyway, my project is going to symbolize the global reach of the Freeze, but how it's personal for all the people across the globe. For me, global is personal, because my family lives all over."

"Ugh. That's so good," Nellie said. She pouted, digging her hands into the pockets of her furry mauve sweater. "Mine isn't that good."

Nellie had already told us about the collage she was making from texts and emails she, Sonya, their mom, and their dad had exchanged since the Freeze had started. I actually really liked her idea—the way they'd used technology to be together when they couldn't be physically.

"Thanks," Priya said. "It was easy, once I thought about what this has all been like for me."

"What's yours on, Lou?" Nellie asked.

"I'm still figuring it out," I said.

"You were supposed to have decided already," Priya said.

Nellie's brown eyes were sharp as a fox's as she focused in on me. "Why didn't your mom help you come up with an idea? Wouldn't it have made sense... art project, artist, you know?"

"She said it's important I come up with my own idea," I said.

It wasn't a lie, but it wasn't the whole truth, either.

If I were honest about what Mom was like now, how she'd been acting, it wouldn't make any sense to them. They knew Mom the way she'd been before: setting up art activities for us on playdates, teaching us to paint stained glass, ordering us pizza, showing us old movies she'd loved, like *Clueless* and *13 Going on 30*, and letting us play with her costume jewelry.

From the other side of the gym, I saw Luke coming toward us.

"Why is he always following you?" Nellie said, her voice an irritated whisper.

I wanted to tell her he was my friend, but I didn't want to make things worse, either.

Luke climbed up onto the riser and sat between Nellie and me. Nellie shifted in her seat and shared a look with Priya.

"What're you guys talking about?" he asked, tossing his bag down on the gym floor.

"Time capsule," Priya said, staring into her book.

"What're you doing for yours?" I said to Luke, who seemed oblivious to the way Priya and Nellie were acting at his arrival.

"Singing a song. One of my dad's," he said.

"With your dad?" Nellie asked, a distance in her voice.

A twisting, sick feeling took over—I couldn't look at Luke.

He stammered for a second, and I thought about cutting him off and changing the subject before he had to answer.

"My dad, he, uh—he had an accident. He can't really…uh…do that kind of thing right now," Luke said, looking down at his shoes.

"Oh," Nellie said. "I didn't know. Sorry."

I was surprised that Nellie sounded genuinely sad for Luke, but I was also worried at the suspicion in her eyes as they rested on me—like I'd kept this secret from her.

Priya frowned, her expression sympathetic as she looked up at Luke from her book. "He'll get better, right?" she asked, and I cringed.

"Yes," I said, my voice sharp.

Luke seemed surprised by my answer, but he followed my lead. "Right. Eventually," he said, sounding a little unsure.

"At least you have an awesome idea. Louisa still

doesn't have one. I said her mom should have helped her come up with something," Nellie said.

"I know. Can you believe Gracie wouldn't even help?" Priya said.

I felt myself tensing up.

"Well, I don't blame her. She's still really sad," Luke said, and he looked at me like we were on the same team.

"What do you mean?" Nellie asked.

"About Louisa's nana," he said.

"What about your nana?" she said.

My throat felt dry. Priya was silent, but her eyes were locked on me, too.

"Uh," I started, but I didn't even know what to say. I looked down at my shoes, my eyes filling with tears. "I—I don't want to talk about it," I stammered, and then I stood up and jumped off the bleachers.

I ran out of the gym and raced down the hall to the bathroom before anyone else could see me. In the bathroom, I threw cold water on my face and stared in the mirror, watching the droplets of water mix with tears and drip down my blotchy cheeks.

The door to the bathroom swung open a few minutes later. I could see Nellie in the mirror; she leaned against the wall and studied me.

"Um, Lou... are you okay?"

I turned to face her.

"My nana died," I said, looking at the wad of paper towel by Nellie's feet.

"I didn't know," Nellie said.

"I didn't want to tell anyone."

"But Luke knew," she said.

"Luke's different," I said, knocking my shoes together. "He lives in my building and he knows my parents really well. And I didn't want him to tell anyone."

"You should have told me. I've met her, right? She was old, right, and she had that white, curly hair?"

I looked at her. "No. She didn't have white hair. And she wasn't *that* old."

Nellie searched my face like she was confused. "Well, I'm sorry... I'm sorry she died," she said.

"Me too."

"I still don't get why Luke is different. You should have told me."

"I—it's hard to talk about," I stammered.

"With *me*," she said. I felt awkward then, like I couldn't look her in the eye. I wanted to disappear.

"No. It's hard to talk about with anyone," I said, and I pushed through the bathroom door.

Luke was standing in the hallway, waiting for me. I motioned for him to follow me away from the bathroom and the gym.

"I—I didn't know," he stammered, once we were alone.

"Know what?"

"That it was a secret. I thought they knew about your nana. I wouldn't have said anything," Luke said.

"It wasn't a *secret*. I just didn't tell them."

"Why not?"

"I don't like to talk about it. You should get it. It's like your dad. Do you like explaining what happened to him?"

"No. But it happened. I'm not going to pretend it didn't," he said.

"I'm *not* pretending. I just don't want you telling people my private business."

"I'm sorry. But they're your friends. I just thought they knew, and I didn't think they were being nice about your mom."

"Well, she's my mom, not yours, and you don't have to say anything about her, or me, or my nana," I said. I blinked tears away and stormed down the hallway to the library, where I sat and cried quietly until the bell that ended recess rang.

I spent the rest of the day avoiding Priya, Nellie, and Luke.

At school, I got to pretend that everything at home was the same as it always had been. I could act like Mom was happy again, and Nana was alive, and no one would say anything about it.

Now Luke was interfering; he knew too much.

～ʃ

That afternoon, Mom and Dad were both waiting for me outside the school's front gates. Dad had started walking to school for pickup with Mom on his nights off. He said he liked spending as much time with us as he could, but I had a sneaking suspicion he was anxious about us getting home safe. Will was jumping around in a pile of snow with one of his little friends. When I reached them, Mom put her hand on my shoulder and Dad pulled my hat down tight over my ears.

"We're walking Luke home, too," he said, and I sighed very loud, clouds blowing out of my mouth in the cold air.

"Where is he?" Mom asked, and I pointed back toward the school exit I'd come from.

Dad gave me a look, like I wasn't being very helpful, before going to collect Luke, and I stared at Mom. I wanted to tell her about what had happened today, and why I was angry, but she seemed preoccupied, staring off into the distance, her face sleepy. Before Nana died, Mom always gave me good advice about friend drama. Now, if she'd noticed I was upset, she wasn't even bothering to say anything.

Luke, Will, and I walked home side by side, taking slow, steady steps behind Mom and Dad. Luke gave me a timid smile when we first began our walk, but I didn't smile back. I guessed he felt guilty, because he was quiet then, except for when Will asked him questions about his favorite parts of the Rodrigo series.

I was trying to hear Mom and Dad, who were having a very snippy conversation. I couldn't hear every word, with the strong wind blowing, but it sounded like Mom said "It was my choice," and I think Dad said, "We can't just exist like this forever."

Then Mom said "I am going through something," and it sounded like Dad responded with "How about me?"

Their words knocked against one another, like rocks pelted against a glass window.

～の

That afternoon, instead of going out to our ice house, I opened up my *Our House* book. I traced Nana's handwriting with my finger, admiring her beautiful cursive. I missed her—the book felt like the last piece of her that I could hold in my hand.

Today I stared at the illustration of the inside of a cave in the first chapter of the book. I'd always skipped it—the caves didn't seem beautiful to me like the houses I studied. But this time I noticed that the cave's walls had brown-and-red ink paintings; one looked like tiger stripes painted over a long oval, and another looked like a group of cows.

People painted on the walls of this cave to capture what life was like then. This room could have served as a nursery or maternity ward, as suggested by the drawings on the wall. By studying the symbolism in cave paintings, we can learn about the cave dwellers, their customs, and their culture from the visual accounts they left behind.

The cave paintings taught us about the people. This made the caves sort of *more* special than any of the other houses in the book. The wall paintings told a story about the lives of the people who lived inside. They were basically a time capsule. And according to the book, the paintings *themselves* were symbolic. I felt a wave of excitement as I stood up and rushed into my parents' bedroom.

"Mom!"

Will was reading a Magic School Bus book aloud to Mom while Dad was folding laundry.

"What?" Mom said.

"Okay, so there are these old caves, from thousands of years ago, and the caves have these paintings on them. They're just like time capsules, because they've existed for a super-long time and they show what life was like back then. And also, they're symbols."

"What's this all about?" Dad asked, but Mom's eyes lit up.

"Lascaux. That's the name of the cave you're talking about?" she said.

"Yeah. I think, something like that. The book said it's in France."

Mom stood up and walked to her bookshelf. "Hey!" Will called after her, and he glared at me.

She opened up a box of old photos. I watched her flip through them until she stopped, her hands fixing on whatever she was looking for.

"Here," she said, walking toward me.

She handed me an old photo. She was standing in a cave just like the ones in the book. She looked young, like she was a teenager, maybe. Nana was at her side.

"What is this?"

"That's Lascaux," Mom said, her voice warm like a hug.

I traced Mom and Nana with my pointer finger. "You went there together?"

"When I was just out of high school. Not to the caves with the original paintings in them, though. You can't go into them anymore—it's not safe for the art. So these are perfect replicas."

"Oh. That's kind of…"

"Disappointing?" she said, and then she shook her head. "No. It was really magical."

"Well, I was thinking that for my time capsule project, I could make a painting like the cave drawings, with all the symbols that would tell someone thousands of years from now what it was like to be here, in our apartment during the Freeze."

"Oh, *that* is perfect," Mom said.

I looked back at the photo of Mom and Nana, their smiles matching. It was almost like Nana had led me to this idea with her book.

Nineteen

"My mom asked me to drop this off."

I stood in front of Luke in his doorway on Sunday night, holding a casserole dish full of lasagna that Mom had cooked earlier.

"Come in," he said, stepping aside so that I would follow.

"Oh no, that's okay. I..."

But he was already calling for Alesha. I stepped inside. We hadn't spoken since our fight at school. We hadn't spent Saturday together in the ice house like we usually did.

Alesha entered wearing sweats. I couldn't remember ever seeing Alesha in something that wasn't elegant.

"So thoughtful," she said, accepting the casserole dish with a smile.

"Did you help your mom? Reminds me of when I was a kid. Whenever something was going on in the neighborhood, if someone was sick or something, my mom would have us make something for them. That's how I learned how to cook! She'd make whatever she thought our neighbors would want, and she'd teach me a new recipe."

Upstairs, Mom was probably still resting after the ordeal this lasagna had caused: She'd burned the first round, which we were going to eat for dinner, and this was the second. She'd told Will and me to stay out of the kitchen, and she'd had to open all the windows so that our fire alarm wouldn't go off a million times, so we were freezing, and Will wouldn't stop whining about it, even after I pulled the blankets off our beds and wrapped us both up in them.

It had been nothing like Alesha's childhood memories.

"Anyway, your dad will love this lasagna, won't he?" Alesha asked Luke.

"Yep," he said, his voice tired.

"I should go," I said.

"Thank your mom for us," Alesha said, putting her hand on my back.

"I'll see you tomorrow," I said, looking at Luke.

"Yeah," he said after I was already heading toward the door.

I was halfway up the stairs to my apartment when Luke called out to me.

"What?" I said, turning and going down the stairs again.

"I really didn't mean to tell Priya and Nellie about your nana. I hope you don't think I can't keep a secret. I'd never tell *anyone* about our house."

"It's okay, Luke," I said. Maybe I'd overreacted. He'd been defending Mom, which was nice of him. I gave him a smile that I hoped made it clear it really was okay, and he nodded.

"My dad's favorite movie is still *Men in Black*," Luke said then, a proud look in his eyes.

"What?"

"He put it on all by himself, and he loved it," he said.

"See? He's getting better. It's working," I said.

"Things'll get better with your mom, too. I know they will," he said.

"*Well*," I said, excited, "something *did* happen."

I told him about my cave painting idea, and he agreed that it was super significant that Mom and Nana had been to the cave together.

The hope in his eyes as he listened made me feel so happy that I practically floated back up the stairs to my apartment.

～৩

That Friday, at Makers Club, we listened to Keisha talk about a new game she'd gotten for her Nintendo Switch that let you build your own buildings as tall as you wanted, and you could decorate them however you wanted and choose the materials.

"That sounds really fun," I said.

"Yeah. My mom got it for me, and I started building out of sand, because it looked so cool to have this huge skyscraper like a sandcastle."

Andre, who clearly had been eavesdropping, butted in. "It would be impossible to create a skyscraper out of sand."

"Well, maybe if it was wet sand…," I said,

thinking of the sandcastles I'd made at the beach every summer.

I noticed Nellie's gaze resting on me from across our table; she had that tortured boredom in her eyes that I felt sometimes when Will made me watch some baby show.

We'd been working on our new model for the past two meetings—so far, we'd represented icicle stakes and beams with plastic forks left over from the cafeteria. We'd reused ice cube trays from our houses to create the factory where ice cube bricks would be manufactured, and we were using clear blocks to represent the ice cube bricks in buildings.

Today we were solving an important problem: How would these ice cubes be transported?

While Jamal and Luke debated whether a truck or a train or a helicopter or some new invention would be best suited to transporting materials, I thought of slippery highways, tires skidding on black ice, cars weaving across lanes.

I tried to put the image out of my brain, but it wouldn't fade. "I think helicopters—but the kind that can land on water. I don't want people driving anymore," I said, interrupting Jamal's statement that trains would probably be the best mode of transportation if they could solve for frozen tracks.

Luke wanted to figure out how to make highways ice-proof. If that were a possibility, wouldn't we have figured it out by now?

Both Luke and Jamal stared at me.

"Why not?" Jamal asked.

"I don't think there'd be a safe enough solution to avoid all those accidents."

"Helicopters are really expensive, and people could still crash in the sky," Luke said. "Sorry, but I don't think that's a good idea."

How were we supposed to solve this, anyway? We were only in sixth grade—all of a sudden, the idea of kids trying to fix these massive problems seemed ridiculous. I stared at Nellie—her eyes were glued to her lap, and I could see her hands moving. I could tell she was sneaking a peek at her phone.

Maybe our project *was* pointless and boring, the way Nellie was making it look right now.

At the end of the meeting, while everyone was putting their coats on and switching from their school shoes into their snow boots, Nellie stood in front of me, her furry coat buttoned up to the collar.

"Hey," she said.

I wrapped my sunflower-colored scarf around my neck. "Hi."

"So, Priya didn't come today," she said, twisting the ends of her hair in circles.

"Yeah. I see."

I'd noticed this right away, but I'd thought maybe she'd had to leave early.

"She didn't want to tell you, but she's not going to come anymore," Nellie said.

I tried to ignore the gnawing feeling of being betrayed, first by Luke, and now by Priya. It felt strange to have her quit without telling me why.

"Oh."

Nellie pursed her lips.

"She could have just told me," I said, shrugging, trying to hide that I was upset.

"Well, she didn't want you to get mad."

"I wouldn't have been. I'm not," I said.

"It's just... she didn't want to hurt your feelings, especially since your grandma died and everything," Nellie said, looking down to the floor, her voice wavering. "But you've been kind of different with us lately."

"What do you mean?" I asked, gripping the edges of my scarf.

I could see Luke watching us out of the corner of my eye, and I felt like everyone could hear, even though Nellie wasn't talking very loudly.

"You're different," she said. "You talk about Makers Club all the time now, and you're not interested in what we talk about." Her cheeks were pink, and she kept blinking and staring at the floor, like she was trying not to cry.

"That's not true. You were both members last year. I didn't make you join."

"But we did it because of you," she said, sounding exasperated. "And, you know, it seems like you don't really care about us ... or ... me," Nellie said, and when she finally looked at me, I realized how upset she was.

"What?"

"All you care about is Luke. You two are always together. And why didn't you even tell me your grandma died? I told you that my family is going to move me to Switzerland, and that my dad is basically starting a totally different family and my mom is stuck in Korea. I told you everything."

Nellie held her hands over her eyes then, and I swallowed hard.

Pretty much everyone had left the classroom. Mr. Rojas was packing his things up at his desk, and I was afraid he'd already heard us. I nodded toward the exit, and Nellie started walking away.

I followed behind her out into the hallway. Through the long windows that lined the hall, I could see Dad standing on the corner waiting to walk Luke and me home.

Nellie held the cords of her backpack and twirled them.

"The only reason I didn't tell you about my nana was because it felt easier not to talk about it. I could pretend it didn't happen," I said. "I can't pretend at home."

"Well, I *really* didn't like Luke having to tell me, like he knows you better than I do."

Then she turned and charged toward the exit. I sprinted after her and caught up. "Wait," I said, grabbing the shiny gold handle of her backpack.

She stopped walking. "What?" she said.

"I'm sorry," I said. "It wasn't on purpose."

"I know," she said, and then bolted out the front

door of the school. I watched her meet Sonya by the gate, and then I trudged toward the west corner, where Dad was waiting with Luke.

I was quiet the whole walk home. Luke didn't ask about Nellie, but he kept stealing looks in my direction and I knew he was curious. I was stunned. I thought *she'd* been acting different with me—that was why I'd had to overthink everything when we talked. Knowing that she thought I'd done something to hurt her was shocking.

It felt like I'd handed in a math test, then realized there was a whole back page I'd skipped.

Twenty

"How *do you* eat that?"

"Like this!" I dipped an Oreo deep into my jar of peanut butter and took a bite. Luke fake-gagged. "What?"

"It's just so slimy."

"It's peanut butter."

"Yeah. But on an Oreo? It's just wrong."

"*You're* just wrong," I said. I took another Oreo from the baggie and dunked it in the peanut butter. "Open wide," I said, moving it toward his mouth in an airplane motion.

"Evil," he said, and he knocked it out of my hand.

"Sorry." I picked it up and ate it anyway, which made Luke grimace.

I shrugged. It was Saturday afternoon, and we'd spent a big part of the morning practicing Brian's old song. My drumming was getting better, and Luke's playing was starting to actually sound a *tiny* bit like Brian's had.

"Anyway, I've been thinking," I said.

"I can just tell you're gonna say something I'm not gonna like."

"That's mean. You don't know that," I said, but I knew he was right.

"Fine. What were you thinking?"

"Well, I was just thinking, what if we just see if your dad can still play guitar?"

"What do you mean, *just see?*"

"Like, we just hand him a guitar, and you see what he does with it," I said.

I didn't like the horrified look on Luke's face.

"You *know* this—they tried to see if he could play in the hospital," Luke said. "It was one of the first things they did with him, once they realized he'd lost his memory. It's his job—so it's super important. And he got really upset. He wouldn't try."

Just then a cold breeze flooded the ice house from outside. I shivered.

Shaking it off, I said, "That was weeks ago now. And it's not like he couldn't play—he just wouldn't, right? Did he even try? I mean, he can still walk and talk. And he's played guitar for so long, I'm sure it's like walking and talking to him."

"I think if he remembered guitar, he would have taken it and tried in the hospital," Luke said. "He never even asks about his guitars, or anything, and he sees them hung up in the hall every day."

I dipped another cookie into peanut butter. "I saw this story the other day on *Wake Up, America*, about this guy who got amnesia, but he'd always been a genius piano player. He could still play! He remembered all of it."

"It's not TV, Louisa."

"It was a true story! We can look it up! His name is Ethan something."

"No. That's one person. Besides, we can't just *make* him try."

Luke started plucking the strings of his guitar. I could see he was annoyed.

"Well, then we'll never know, Luke. Maybe it's

not as complicated as we're making it. Maybe the ceiling just shows us the future, and if we just trust that, we can make it come true. So maybe we just bring him his guitar and ask him to play for *you*, and maybe it'll work."

"Look, I get that you're trying to help, but it's… it's not really your business how I decide to deal with *my* dad and what *I'm* seeing."

"But—I mean, I know he's not my dad, but he's— he's Brian! It's important to me, too."

"You think I'm just going to do what you tell me to because you want me to do it? You don't know *everything*, you know."

My face was hot. "I didn't say I knew everything. I never said that."

"Well, remember when you told me not to tell people your business? This is my business, not yours. You should stay out of mine and start thinking about your own."

"I am thinking about mine…," I started, but he talked over me.

"You say your vision is you seeing your mom the way she was before."

"Yeah, so?"

"How are you going to make that happen?"

I swallowed hard. My ears felt hot, even though I'd taken my hat off.

I thought of those scenes on the beach: The Freeze was over, and Mom was happy. It seemed like having the Freeze end would fix things for her.

"Well, obviously I can't just make the snow melt."

"What does that have to do with anything?" Luke said.

"It has *everything* to do with her."

"She's like this now because her mom died, Louisa. Not the Freeze," Luke said, and I knew he was right. Aside from forcing her to have hope, though, there wasn't anything I could do to change things for her.

"Well, her mom died *because* of the Freeze, so it's related," I said.

I didn't know why I was even fighting with him— I *wanted* help. I wanted him to tell me what to do to make my plan work. "The only thing I know I can do is let her see that things are going to get better— that she'll be happy again. The one way I know how to do that is the way it happened for me: in the house."

"What? You want to bring her here?" he said, narrowing his eyes.

It was only dawning on me then, as I heard him say this out loud; it could be the only thing that would give her hope—seeing the future with her own eyes.

"Just listen. What if we just let her look into the ceiling *once*? She'll see her future. It'll give her hope. She'll see that things will be okay. Maybe it'll fix everything.... Maybe she'll be able to move on."

"No," Luke said, speaking over me.

"I *know* it's just ours. I get that. But—I mean, Luke, you see what she's like. It would help her," I said.

She was like a wilting flower, and the vision in the ice house could be like the sun streaming down and reviving her, helping her bloom.

"It's not for her. It's only for us, and you know that. That's the rule," he said.

"I would do it for you," I said, my voice cracking.

For a whole minute we sat there without saying a word, both of us staring at the icy ground.

"It's a bad idea, Louisa."

"Why?" I said, my voice small.

"It's not going to work for her, because she's not a kid, and this won't be just *ours* anymore. And the magic won't work anymore."

"You have *no* idea if that's true," I said.

"I have *some* idea."

"How? You don't know that."

"If it was *for* other people, things like this would be happening all over the place. But it's not. It's only happening to us."

"That's not a good reason," I said, raising my voice. "I keep trying to think of new ways to help your dad—I'd try anything to help him. You're not just *not* helping me, you're trying to stop me from fixing my mom." Luke was silent.

I picked my hat out of my pocket, where I'd shoved it, and put it back on. "Maybe you're fine just sitting around waiting to see if your dad ever gets better, but I'm not. I'm going to fix my mom. And maybe it is a risk, but at least I'll know," I said, and I stormed out of our house on my knees.

$\backsim$

At school that Monday morning, I waited anxiously for Nellie in the cafeteria.

"Hey," Priya said, plopping down on the bench beside me.

"Did Nellie say anything to you?"

She looked a little uncomfortable then. "Sorry about Makers Club. I just—I was afraid to talk to you about it. I didn't wanna stay late on a Friday when I don't really care about that stuff as much anymore."

I shook my head. "You could have told me. It's okay," I said, hoping I was doing a good job of hiding my resentment.

"Oh. Okay," Priya said. "Well, what do you mean, then? What would Nellie have said to me?"

I shrugged. "Nothing."

"Okay, then," Priya said, like she didn't really believe me, and she started fussing inside her backpack. After a minute, she pulled out *Rodrigo and the Moon: Book Two*. "This is really good," she said, before opening up to a page in the middle of the book and beginning to read. I didn't even know she'd read book one. I thought of Luke and looked down at my fingernails.

A few minutes later, Nellie marched toward us in furry white boots, drenched from the sidewalk snow.

I jumped up from my seat and rushed over to her before she could reach our table—I wanted to talk without Priya listening in.

"I'm sorry," I said, once she was in earshot.

Nellie had a hollow look on her face. "I don't know why I got so upset," she said.

"I wasn't trying to keep things from you."

"You didn't have to keep *anything* from me."

"I don't want you to be mad at me," I said.

"Let's just forget about it," she said, and she gave me a smile that didn't match her eyes before walking toward Priya.

Priya closed her book as Nellie slipped onto the bench opposite her. I sat down in my seat again and told myself that everything was fine with Nellie now, but I had a feeling it was a lie.

"Maude B released a new video. Sonya showed me," Nellie said.

"Wait! Wait! I have to tell you—I finished the season!" Priya announced.

Nellie squealed, and I nodded, trying to sound enthusiastic like they did, but I couldn't help thinking that no matter how much I tried, something had shifted among the three of us. I wanted to go home and hide under the covers of my bed.

Twenty-One

After school that evening, I found Will sitting in my window seat, his face pressed up against the windowpane.

"What's in there?" he said, pushing the top of his finger against the glass until his fingertip turned white, pointing to the ice house.

"Nothing," I said.

"Why won't you let me go in?"

I bit my lip. "Luke and I agreed we wouldn't let anyone else in. I'm sorry. I made a promise."

"It's not fair. You're not even using it right now!"

"Will, come on. I'll build something with you. We can use one of your new Lego sets," I said.

He glared at me, and before I could stop him he was running down the hallway screaming, "Mom!"

That afternoon, Mom had told me she had a headache and needed to take a nap. She'd asked me to watch Will for a while. Now here he was, making even more noise than usual, fighting with me.

"Leave her alone," I said, chasing him. I tried to grab his arm, but he ignored me and slammed up against Mom's bedroom door.

He stopped after the door swung open. Mom was sitting up in her bed.

"What is it?" Mom usually tried to be softer with Will, but her voice was sharp and cold now.

"Louisa won't let me play in her house," he whined.

"It's not yours," Mom said. She was taking my side for once, but it didn't feel good the way I thought it would.

Will's chin began shaking. "*Mommy.*"

"Don't start. Not today," she said. She rolled over, her back to us now. Will was sitting in the doorway, pulling himself into a ball like a kitten.

"Will," I said, bending down to talk to him. "Let's go play. In the front yard," I added quickly, to make sure he didn't think he was getting in the ice house.

He didn't perk up the way he usually did, but after another minute, he followed me into the foyer, where we both bundled up.

It was dusk outside. The sky was the color of a melted rainbow ice, the dark red and purple and blue fading together. The setting sun cast a purple shadow over the snow, a bit of light still peeking through the buildings across the street.

The zombie trees looked almost friendly, like guards of our front-yard fortress.

Mom and I had watched baby Ama for Mr. and Mrs. Owusu while they'd taken their turn shoveling the front walk last weekend, but new snow had already started filling up the path they'd cleared.

"What should we play?" I asked, but Will was ahead of me. He took a few giant steps, fighting his way through the snow.

I held my mitten-covered hands to my mouth to hide my snickering. It looked like he was walking through a wave, the snow sputtering on either side of him as he battled against it. Snow particles flew in bursts past us both as Will turned to look at me, his orange hat hanging off his head.

"Pull your hat down!" I said.

He laughed as he fixed his hat, even as the wind knocked against him.

"Wanna race me?" I asked.

At this idea, Will jumped up in the snowbank and started cheering. "That tree there can be the finish line," he said, pointing at one of the dying trunks at the far end of the lawn.

As I trudged through the snow to the starting point—the fence of snow along the front of our building—I pulled the collar of my parka up over my neck and held it closed.

Will huffed and puffed next to me, hopping from foot to foot.

"You ready?" I asked, taking a sort of lunge position in the thick snow that came up to my knees.

"Ready!"

"On your mark, get set, go!" I called out. I let Will get a tiny head start, counting to five before I began moving.

The legs of my ski pants rubbed against each other, making an awful crinkling sound. It was so hard to move that I might as well have been wearing steel armor; I felt frozen in place, anyway.

Will was making a little more progress, forcing

his way with huge hops into the snow. He was falling forward, which wasn't a terrible strategy.

I kept trying to trudge against this force—this unmovable wall—until there was a loud gust of wind. I stood there frozen, looked up at the purple-blue sky, stared at the first few stars beginning to shine, and howled into it.

At first, Will must have thought the noise was just the wind, but a second later he turned and looked at me.

I was cupping my hands around my mouth, and howling, hollering into the air.

This sky that kept raining down on us, bringing snow we couldn't shovel, ice we couldn't melt—it had taken so much from us and just didn't seem to care. Screaming as loud as I could, with no words, I exhaled anger and sadness and frustration until there was nothing left in my chest but cold air.

Will wasn't moving forward anymore, just watching me and laughing, maybe a little nervously.

After my screaming was over, I let out a huff of relief.

"You win," I said.

Will wasn't far ahead of me—there was no way

he was going to make it to the finish-line tree—but he seemed to have forgotten the destination anyway.

He cheered, and I watched him bounce up and down in the snow.

I leapt forward, grabbing his leg. Landing with my back in the snow, I sank down into it a little, and Will grabbed my arm like he would if we were actually floating in water, afraid that we might be separated.

We both stared up at the sky, shivering against the snow.

"The Little Dipper," Will said. When he lifted his arm, his coat squeaked, and we both laughed.

"That's not the Little Dipper," I said, my words chattering like my teeth.

"It's really cold," Will said, sitting up.

"Ready to go in?" I asked. Will jumped up even faster than me.

At the front door, he turned around. "Good night, snow," he said, his voice like a robot's.

"Good night, Will," I said, in a squeaky mouse voice. Will laughed really hard then, shaking his head.

I stood in our building doorway and took one last look outside. The street was deserted, and it was dark now, no last traces of the sun or fading rainbow colors in sight. The moon hung above us, keeping watch.

∼෨

"So if I do move to Switzerland," Nellie said at lunchtime, pulling out a shiny brochure with a picture of a very blue lake on the cover, "this will be my school. My *college*: that means high school."

"It's beautiful," I said, and Nellie beamed.

I was being extra cautious and nice with Nellie ever since our fight at Makers Club. She, on the other hand, had been acting like she wanted me to feel left out. She talked about things I wasn't a part of in front of me, like FaceTime calls she and Priya hadn't included me in, or stories on Maude B's Instagram she knew I didn't follow.

"You need to finish middle school first," Priya said, and then she took a huge bite of her granola bar.

"They do things different there. I'd be going to *college*," Nellie said.

She opened up the brochure and laid it out on the table in front of us. "Here is the indoor swimming pool, and here are the horse trails," she said, pointing to each photo. The edge of her ring, which looked like a seashell, clacked against the paper each time she touched it. "And there, that's the café. A fancy chef makes these hot meals for everyone every day."

Our cafeteria was gray and smelled like disinfectant. For school lunch, you could get sandwiches or, once in a while, pizza.

There was no question: *College* sounded way cooler than middle school. Nellie took a sip of her water and stared from Priya to me like she was waiting for some huge reaction to her school tour.

"I wish our school were like this," I said, hopeful that this was what she wanted to hear.

She just nodded, though, and turned her attention back to Priya, who was reading again. I wondered if Priya was worried about what life would be like if Nellie really *did* move.

"Pri-ya," Nellie said then, staring daggers in her direction. "Did you see Maude B's Insta stories last night?"

I shifted uncomfortably on the bench, wishing Priya would say no for once so I wouldn't be the odd one out.

"Yes!" Priya squealed, and I smiled in an awkward way.

"What was it?" I said, trying to insert myself in their conversation.

"Why don't you go ask your boyfriend?" Nellie said.

Priya looked startled.

"Huh?" I said.

"Oh, Luke doesn't know anything about Maude B?" Nellie asked, and I felt stung by her sarcasm.

"He's not my boyfriend," I said.

"Well, then why is he always hanging around you?" she said.

I felt a lump forming in my throat. "He's not," I said, and I swallowed hard, trying to stop the tears I felt pressing against my eyelids.

"They're friends," Priya said, her voice wavering a little.

They didn't know that Luke wasn't speaking to me at the moment, and I didn't bother to correct them.

"Yeah. Well, if you're such good friends with Luke, clearly you don't need to pretend *we're* still friends," Nellie said, her eyes cold like marbles.

"Nellie," Priya said, and I could tell from her voice that she didn't want things to escalate like this.

"I'm *not* pretending," I said.

"It's fine. It's no one's fault. I have Priya, and you can have Luke," Nellie said.

She stood up, swinging her backpack on, and gestured for Priya to follow.

Priya seemed to hesitate before she got up from the bench, but only for a second. Then they were gone, and I was alone at the cafeteria table, crying for everyone to see.

∽

The rest of the week passed in a lonely wave. That Friday, without Nellie, Priya, or Luke at Makers Club, I had to bite my lip to keep from crying at the sinking sadness I felt.

To make matters worse, Mom's bleak mood continued all week.

By Sunday, I couldn't take it—I felt like I was catching her bad energy. That morning, she shuffled into the kitchen like a sleepwalker. She was silent while her coffee brewed, staring out the window with tired eyes.

When she sat next to me at the table, mug of coffee in hand, her face looked puffy, like she'd been crying. "Why haven't you been out in the yard with Luke the past few days?"

I was surprised she'd noticed, but I couldn't talk to her about my fight with him since it was *about* her, so I just shrugged.

"That little house, it's all very secretive," she said before taking a sip of her coffee. Her eyes looked brighter.

"It's not a secret," I said.

"No?"

"Nope."

"But it's just for you and Luke. Got it," she said. Her sudden interest in our house and the lightness of her voice felt like a sign.

"Mom?"

"Uh-huh," she said, holding her mug to her mouth.

"I want to show you something."

"Okay. Sure. What is it?"

I could tell she was only half listening. She yawned and started scraping something off the table with her finger.

"I want to bring you out to the ice house."

Mom's eyes widened. "I thought only you and Luke could go inside?"

"Well, I just want to show you. It's not a big deal," I lied. My heart was racing.

"Well, if you're sure. Yeah. I'll go out and look," she said, and then she took another long sip of her coffee.

She didn't seem especially excited, which was disappointing, but then I thought that the element of surprise would make it even more wonderful for her when she looked up at the ceiling and saw that things were going to be all right.

∾

"I don't think I'm gonna fit in here so easily."

I had crawled inside before her, and now she was shimmying through the doorway. She was still wearing her pajamas—she'd thrown her coat on top of them—and her hair was tangled, tucked under her collar. She still looked half asleep as she made her way inside.

She ducked her head down a little so that it wouldn't hit the curve of the wall, and scanned the house.

"Wow," she said, looking from the walls up to the ceiling.

I felt her eyes linger on the piece of *Teardrop* pressed on the top of the archway. I hadn't thought about how she might react to seeing it here. But when she looked at me, she smiled and said, "You know who would love this? Nana."

I hoped she was right. I thought of Nana squeezing inside and looking all around—I could picture her laughing and then worrying that someone would need to carry her out of there.

Mom continued to inspect, touching the walls with her gloved fingers, an awestruck look in her eyes.

It seemed so tiny with an adult inside.

"This is incredible. Really," she said, and I believed her. But I was preoccupied.

"I want to show you something else."

"Okay. What?"

I lay down on the ground and began to demonstrate our angel-making routine.

"Just do this, and look up at the ceiling."

She watched me, confused. "What?"

"I just—I want you to try it."

"I'm going to get soaking wet."

"Please? Just trust me."

"Fine. Fine. Okay. Here I go," she said.

She lay back, and I watched her copy me, first really slowly and then a little bit faster, lifting her head to check that I was still shifting in the snow.

"Now look up at the ceiling."

Her eyes settled on the ceiling as she continued her movements, but not with as much excitement as me.

"Do I just—I just keep doing it?"

"Just . . . a little longer."

She continued another minute, and then she sat up. I sat up, too.

"Did you see anything?" I asked.

"There are sparkles up there—like glitter? Is that what you're talking about?" She looked over at me, and I sensed that she could tell I was disappointed by her response. "Wow. It's so beautiful. How'd you do that?"

I knew how hard she was trying to make me feel like she was seeing what I wanted her to see. That made it worse.

"It just happened like that," I said, giving her a sad smile.

"I'm really proud that you took all the snow and the ice and you used it to make something *so* wonderful. It's inspiring," she said. "It's such a special place. Thanks for letting me see."

It *had been* a very special place. Luke had been right—I'd just ruined it.

Twenty-Two

After the disappointment with Mom, I couldn't face going into the ice house. So the following afternoon, I turned the wobbly kitchen table into my art studio. I set out a tall blank canvas I'd found in the linen closet, along with Mom's drawing pencils and a set of her acrylic paints and brushes. I filled a cup with water and left it next to the paints. I also opened up my book to the pages of Lascaux for some inspiration.

One of the photos from the cave was labeled *Hall of Bulls*, with yellow and red outlines of bulls and horses covering the wall. The book told me that over nine hundred of the cave paintings included animals, but animals hadn't been a part of the Freeze; at least not for me.

I made a list of things I thought about when I thought about the Freeze:

>*Nana*
>
>*Ice*
>
>*Snow*
>
>*Our ice house*
>
>*Brian's memory*
>
>*Luke's guitar*
>
>*Hot chocolate*
>
>*The wall of heat that hits you when you*
>*   open the door to our apartment*
>
>*The smell of chicken cooking in the kitchen*
>
>*Supermarket Sweep*

I stood over the table, took one of Mom's art pencils, and began to trace on the canvas. It felt bumpy underneath the graphite, so the sketch I started was ragged at the edges.

Icicles hanging off the branches of our dead trees in the front yard, our ice house like a boulder on a ski slope—I sketched those easily. But I couldn't draw Nana, or a smell, or heat. Even ice was a challenge—clear like glass, but slick and shiny in the moonlight.

I stared at what I'd sketched so far. The outline of our trees with icicles hanging off met my horizon line. The ice house was just past it, on the far right of the canvas.

I took a step back, the way I'd seen Mom do so many times, to get a better look at my work.

As I stared at it, I felt tense, thinking of how much I was missing. How could I capture things I couldn't see?

"Whoa."

Mom stood in the doorway, an empty mug in her hand. She leaned against the doorjamb and tilted her head, narrowing her eyes to give the sketch a critical look.

"I took your supplies," I said.

Without answering, she stepped closer to me.

"The perspective on this is off," she said, pointing to the third and fourth trees. I'd drawn the sidewalk beneath them and planned to paint black ice on it somehow, when I got to the painting phase.

"Huh?"

"Let me?" she said, and she reached for the pencil I was still holding.

She closed one eye and stood back. Then, in a slightly darker stroke, she outlined the sidewalk and the trees again.

"See?" she said, using the pencil to point from the horizon line to the edge of the sidewalk, and then up to the tree. "You have to make sure you have the right perspective. So, if you think about the horizon and where everything is placed in relation to that spot right there…," she went on, pointing to a dot she'd made a little darker on the horizon line. "It's a really small tweak, but it makes such a difference."

She was right—just readjusting the alignment of the trees and the sidewalk helped the sketch look more realistic.

"Thanks," I said, staring up at her as her eyes stayed locked on the canvas.

She nodded at me then, and I felt like I'd pulled her away from something—like dragging her out of a pool before she was ready to dry off.

Then, her voice quiet, she said, "What are your symbols?"

"Oh," I said, and I sat down at the table. She sat down next to me. "Well, there are some things I can't figure out how to draw."

"Like what?"

"Like—the symbols, I guess."

"Wanna tell me what they are?" she asked, almost like this was an obvious next step—except she hadn't wanted to help me. Had she forgotten?

"Well, like one thing that sticks out when I think about the Freeze is how whenever you come inside, the heat is like a wall right in your face."

"Right. It's almost like a blanket that's too fuzzy, right? It can make you itchy."

"Uh-huh," I said.

"So, what if you drew that? A fuzzy blanket—and that could symbolize how . . . well, you tell me. What would that symbolize?"

"Uh, well, I guess it would actually *be* a blanket, but it would symbolize that, like, even though being inside is warmer, and more comfortable than being outside during the Freeze, it can be . . . overwhelming? Like, suffocating, sort of?"

"Yeah. I like that," Mom said.

"I could make the outline of our building, and I could have the blanket spilling out the front door."

"I love that," she said.

I reached for the pencil, and in the far right, behind the ice house, I drew the outline of our building stretching almost all the way to the top of the canvas. Then I marked where our door would be, and I sketched the outline of a blanket, coming out of the doorway.

"Really nice, Lou. Any other symbols you wanna talk through?" Mom asked.

Nana popped into my mind, but I didn't want to jinx this—Mom wanting to help—by depressing her. So I just shook my head. "Not now," I said.

"All right. Well, when you do start painting—and it's fine if you use these," she said, pointing to her good paints with a look that acknowledged I'd taken them without asking, "I suggest you don't do it on this table. You don't want that leg moving and spilling things."

"Oh. Right."

"I can help you set up a better spot tomorrow. Unless you want to get started tonight?"

"Yeah, I wasn't going to start painting yet. I'm still…"

"Getting your ideas out?" she said.

"I guess."

I heard a sound like rocks rattling around in a box then—hail was pelting against the kitchen window. It was a good opportunity to change the subject.

"Do you think the Freeze is going to stop? Or do you think it's just the beginning of an ice age?"

She took the box of paints off the table and started playing with the screw-top caps, checking to make sure they were all on tight.

"You know, it's a different story all the time. It's hard to know what to believe," she said, her voice sounding as tired of the Freeze as I felt.

"So this could be it?"

"What do you mean, *it*?" She unscrewed the blue cap and took the paper towel I'd laid out for my brushes, scraping the dried paint off the edge.

"Like, for the rest of our lives, we'll be living through an ice age, and all the vegetation will die, and people will die, and whole cities will freeze over and be destroyed? And we'll never be able to just go out again for fun? Like to the movies, or the mall, or the park, or something? Or go on vacation?"

"Not unless it's essential travel," Mom said, switching to the green paint and continuing her cleaning process.

"What?!"

"I'm just teasing," she said, looking at me for a second.

"Ha, ha," I said, and I rolled my eyes.

"Listen. Either the Freeze is going to end, or it's not. And either way, we're going to wake up every day and live our lives."

"How are we going to do that, if it's never back to normal?"

Mom dropped the paint back into its box.

"It's like with Nana," she said, closing the top of the box. "In the beginning, remember those first few days, when we kept waking up and we'd forgotten? We couldn't believe she was gone."

"I kept thinking it was a dream, and then I'd realize..." I trailed off.

"Right. But then, after some time passes, it's still hard to accept but eventually you do. Because there's nothing you can do to change it. You can be sad, and it's hard, and you might cry sometimes, but you get through it," Mom said.

"Like you, now?" I asked.

"Well, maybe," she said, looking a little surprised. "But one day, you wake up, and it's just a part of your life—it's not the first thing you think about. You think about other things. Like how lucky you are to have people you love around you. Or a funny movie you saw. Or a book you're reading."

"But I don't want my old life to be something that's like that, though, like it's dead," I said. The possibility of the way everything used to be fading away into something I remembered less and less over time terrified me. I didn't *want* to learn to accept that.

"You don't have an *old* life. You have a life: your family, your friends, the things you love, the things you hate, the things that make you laugh. It's just in a different container right now."

"Well, I want my original container back," I said.

Mom laughed.

"I was being serious, you know," I said.

"I know. Sometimes you just crack me up."

∽

Instead of going to the cafeteria for lunch the next day, I went to the science lab and worked on our model. Mr. Rojas didn't mind—he graded papers and

I built. I didn't tell him I was there because I didn't want to eat lunch all by myself in the cafeteria, now that I was basically friendless.

I was disappointed that Priya hadn't even said anything to me since Nellie had decided we weren't friends anymore; but I was more afraid that now that I'd totally betrayed the privacy of our ice house, Luke would never be my friend again.

I wanted people to be able to read my mind: for Luke to understand that I hadn't felt like I'd had any other choice; for Nellie to realize that it was hard for me to tell her things I knew she wouldn't get. I didn't want her to reject me for the worries I had, for my sadness over the things I missed. Everyone else seemed to be able to accept the way things were now. Even with our Marvelous Metropolis project, I hadn't wanted to accept that the Freeze was our future, but everyone else in Makers Club had been fine doing it.

As I squeezed a long, squiggly tube into the side of one of our ice-cube-composed hospital buildings, I heard someone at the door.

"Hey, can I help, Mr. Rojas?"

"Sure, Luke," Mr. Rojas said.

Luke walked over to the table I was sitting at, and I felt my heart start to race.

"Hi," I said, and he nodded at me.

He sat down across from me and started to fiddle with the archway he'd created out of pipe cleaners. It led to the entrance of a huge park we'd designed to have an ice-safe monorail train around the perimeter. We'd agreed this would be the main form of transportation in our new city.

After an appropriately awkward silence hung between us for a few minutes, I stole a glance at him.

"What're you doing here?" I said, my voice low so that Mr. Rojas wouldn't hear.

"This is my project, too. Not just yours."

"I know," I said. "But you didn't come to Makers Club last week. I'm just surprised you're here during lunch."

"I didn't know you'd be here," he said.

We worked silently for another minute, and then, right when I thought it might be okay to say something normal to him, the way I would have before our fight, he started talking to me.

"You know, ever since you brought your mom in, my guitar playing has gotten worse," he said.

"What?"

"I saw you two go out there the other day. I heard you from my room, and I watched, and ever since then, I can't play my dad's song anymore. When I went into the house after she'd been in there I sounded terrible, like I'd never even practiced it before."

"That *can't* be true," I said, my voice loud enough for Mr. Rojas to look up from his work and stare over at us.

"Well, it is. I was playing because of the magic, and now you killed it by bringing her in there."

"There's no way you could just forget how to play it—you've been practicing all the time. It's gotta be in your head."

"We *know* it's possible to forget how to play," he said.

"Not for a *fact*," I said, and he looked furious then.

I grabbed my bag and left in a huff. I didn't like him bringing Brian up—or blaming Mom for his own bad guitar playing.

∼୬

That night, Dad visited Brian after dinner and came back upstairs looking upset.

"I don't get it—he was really starting to retain things. It felt like he was the Brian I'd known back in high school. He knew lyrics to his favorite songs, and he was cracking jokes with me...but how can he click with me, act like my old friend, and then forget his own son?"

"What do you mean?" I asked. I was mad at Luke, but I was still concerned about him and Brian. *And* I was beginning to worry that Luke was right. Had bringing Mom into the ice house really interfered with his guitar playing?

Maybe even with Brian's progress, too?

"Luke came in to say hi, and when he leaves, Brian says, *Who's that?*"

I felt sick, picturing this. Luke was obsessing over learning Brian's old song, doing everything he could to help his dad get his memory back. But Brian wasn't even registering Luke or any of his hard work.

Mom looked from Dad to me. "It's *one* thing that happened," she said. "It doesn't mean he's not making progress. Recovery's never totally smooth. It's just a bad day. He probably just got confused. His brain is working in overdrive."

Dad rubbed his temples. "It's been a bad week...."

He's been getting frustrated—yelling at Alesha, yelling at Luke. He was *never* like that." Dad's voice was full of discouragement.

"He's scared—he has no idea what's going on," Mom said.

None of us did, so if that were true, we could all be yelling all the time.

But my thoughts turned to Luke then. Maybe he'd come looking for me today in the science lab because even though he was mad at me, he needed a friend.

After school the next day, I stayed bundled up in all my layers and went straight out to our house.

I could tell Luke wasn't inside; there were no footprints leading to the doorway.

Sitting in the center of the house, my legs folded crisscross in front of me, I looked around. This was what I'd imagined before Luke got involved: my own oasis. The rattling wind outside blew through a bit, and I felt the chill even under all my layers.

I lay down and began my snow-angel motions again. As the first sparkling particles of snow shifted in front of me, I relaxed.

Now I was walking along the waves, stepping over seashells, tiptoeing barefoot in the surf. Dad was giving Will a piggyback ride, and Mom was walking next to me, her hand in mine. I guessed this was after we'd been running on the beach—Mom must have caught up with me.

I could almost feel the warmth of the sun as I watched the four of us, glowing in its light. Mom stared up at the sky, the sun beating down on her face. Just then, Will jumped off Dad's back and started running. I chased after him while Mom and Dad watched, laughing.

From reality, I heard something different: the shuffling of knees on thickly packed ice. I turned to look at the entrance.

"Oh." Luke was hovering just inside on his knees, his mouth hanging open.

I sat up, straightening my pom-pom hat and pulling it down over my ears. "You can come in," I said.

He scooted in a little bit, still lingering near the exit.

"Can we talk?" I said, pulling at the edges of my gloves.

"What about?"

"About everything . . . you know . . . our fight?"

He crawled a bit closer. "Fine. What do you want to say?" he said.

My palms were sweating under my gloves. I felt my breath rattling around sharp in my chest.

"You were right. It didn't work. And—I don't want us to be in a fight anymore," I blurted. I felt my cheeks growing hot.

He looked surprised.

"I know why you're mad at me, but . . . I didn't mean to say anything about your dad that would make things worse. I really was just trying to help," I said. "And my mom—she's been really bad. I was desperate to try something. But like I said, you were right. I shouldn't have brought her in."

Luke started picking at the laces of his boots.

"I never know how to help," I said.

The words felt heavy as they tumbled out of my mouth. I wasn't sure he could really understand what I meant.

"How to help *me*?" He scooted a little closer then, finally meeting my eyes.

"Anyone," I said, and with my gloved pointer finger I traced circles onto the snowy floor under me.

"What do you mean?"

I shook my head. "It's not important. I'm sorry for bringing my mom out here. I was just..."

"I get what you were trying to do," Luke said, his eyes warming, and relief poured over me like a sprinkle of fresh snow. "And I think you're wrong. You're good at helping people."

I shrugged. "I think I make things worse."

"Well, you want to help, and that's a big deal. And you try to help, which is really all you can do," he said. His practical, calm advice sounded just like something Alesha would say.

"It makes my mom mad sometimes when I try to make her feel better. And when I try to help with Will, she doesn't even notice," I said.

"My mom doesn't notice anything anymore—good or bad," he said.

"What do you mean?"

"She's too busy worrying about my dad. The other day she asked me to just put the laundry in for her. So I accidentally put one of my red socks in the hot-water load and most of the stuff got all pink. I just put it all in the dryer, because I didn't want her to yell, and she hasn't said anything."

"What was in there?"

"Sheets, and towels, and pajamas, and this fluffy white bathrobe she wears when it's cold."

"You really think she just didn't notice?"

Alesha was pretty calm, but she was sharp—she noticed everything. I couldn't imagine her looking past an entire basket of pink laundry.

"Well, she wore the bathrobe the other morning. Didn't say anything." He raised an eyebrow, and I started giggling.

"The worst part is that she *hates* pink," he added, and we both burst out laughing.

Twenty-Three

$\int$ crabble was Luke's idea.

We'd practiced Brian's song what felt like a thousand times out in our house that afternoon. It was the first week of June, and Luke didn't say it, but I had a feeling that the intensity of his practicing had something to do with Brian's former confidence that the Freeze would be over by his birthday, which was quickly approaching.

Luke's playing sounded as good as it had before I'd brought Mom into the house: definitely not amazing, but the song was recognizable. As grateful as I was that we'd made up, and to see that I hadn't actually killed the magic by bringing Mom into our house, I was growing tired of drumming the same beat over and over again.

After our practice, I was ready for dinner, and homework, and maybe an episode of *Supermarket Sweep*. But Luke had asked if I wanted to play, and once I'd agreed (a little unenthusiastically), he'd met me at the door to my apartment with the game box in his hands and suggested that we invite Will to join.

Clearly, Luke didn't know anything about little brothers.

"That's not a word," I said, pointing to the tiles Will had just flipped over. *B-E-R-N*.

"It is! Like, that is a *burn!*"

"Well, actually, you spell *burn* with a *u* instead of an *e*, Will."

"Nope! I'm right," Will said, grabbing the little black bag with the remaining letter pieces in it and shaking it around.

"Well, maybe we'll take one point off. To be fair," Luke said.

"That's not fair," Will said, pouting.

"Actually, Luke's being super nice, because you're cheating. You needed a *u*," I said.

"Well, I *had* a *u*," Will said. He stared at me, his big hazel eyes full of confusion.

"You should have used it instead of the *e*, then," I said, laughing.

"Maybe just change it out now," Luke said, and he started laughing, too.

Will switched the *e* and the *u*.

"I like this game," he said. "Why don't we play it more?"

When Luke invited him to play, Will had informed us that he was a Scrabble expert. It became clear almost immediately that he had no idea how the game worked.

"We played it at my dad's birthday last summer," Luke said, his voice flat.

"Right. On the beach," I said.

"Your dad said the Freeze would be over by his birthday," Will said, his voice a little gentler than usual.

Luke turned a letter tile between his fingers.

"I remember," he said, and he rubbed his lips together. "But I guess he was wrong."

I'd been avoiding asking Luke about what Dad had said. I didn't like to think about Brian yelling at him or Alesha, or about the fact that he was hardly remembering anything, even after being back at home, surrounded by his family.

"Do you think your dad remembers me yet?" Will asked.

"Will!" I said, horrified by the question, but Luke didn't seem offended. "No, buddy. I don't think he remembers anything from before his accident," he said.

"But he remembers you," Will said.

"No," Luke said.

"Yes. Since he came home—he remembers you since then, right?"

"Well, yeah. But that's not the same thing," Luke said, a little annoyance slipping through his voice.

"It's better than having to explain who you are every day," Will said.

"I guess that's true," Luke agreed. I was relieved to see he wasn't upset.

"Is he still funny?" Will asked.

It sounded like an afterthought, but Luke's eyes lit up at the question. "Actually, yeah. Kind of. He is. Like the other day, he was sitting in the living room watching TV, and some sitcom was on, one of those shows with the laugh track that really isn't funny at all, and I came in and sat with him. He turned to me and said, 'Please tell me I didn't like this show.' He'd always hated it, and when I told him that, he said, 'Oh, thank goodness. I was getting worried when your mom put it on for me. So she's the one with bad taste in TV.'"

I gave Luke an encouraging nod. I recognized the Brian in Luke's story. I knew he did, too.

"My turn!" Will squealed then, as he began to rearrange the tiles on his tile holder.

I rolled my eyes. In Will's world, it was always his turn.

～੭

That night, after Luke went downstairs, I laid old, crinkling pages of newspaper on top of the living room carpet. Mom's art supplies were lined up on the coffee table: her paintbrushes, water cup, tubes of acrylic paint, palette for color mixing.

"You've got to stay away from this whole area," I said, waving my arms around my coffee table, newspaper, canvas workspace.

"I won't go near it!" Will squeaked, as if outraged by my request.

I wanted to ask him to leave, but I could tell he wouldn't—he wanted to stay and see what I was doing.

I looked down at the sketches on my canvas. Pieces of my life reflected back at me. Ms. Lee said symbols were objects that stood for something else—an idea, a feeling, a thought. So far, the only thing that really meant much was the fuzzy blanket escaping out the door to our building.

The biggest piece about the Freeze, the thing that was missing from the canvas, was Nana. Except there was no symbol that could represent her. It was like she was a song, and I was trying to capture her in a single note.

She was warmth on a cold day. She would be a symbol that would illuminate everything else in the painting—she was light.

I dipped my brush into the water and swirled it around. I mixed dots of blue and green and purple together on the palette, and I began to paint—just like those cave dwellers had thousands of years ago.

Something happened as my hand moved against the canvas. It felt like I was losing something heavy and finding something light.

Will stood and watched me paint for a while. He hovered over me, tilting his head up and down like he was grading my work.

At some point, he left to take a bath.

In the background, I heard Dad switch the channel on the TV. The familiar theme song of *Supermarket Sweep* filled the living room. I heard it, but I didn't really take it in. The only thing that mattered was capturing the colors on the canvas, aligning the shadows just right.

∽

"You've got to leave the rest until tomorrow."

"Huh?"

I looked up, my neck stiff from staring at the floor for hours. Dad shook his head. "It's late. Pick this up tomorrow."

"I'm almost done," I said.

He stood up from the couch and walked over.

"Lou!"

I couldn't remember ever having really *shocked* Dad. Not the way he looked now, at least.

"You did this? This whole thing?"

I didn't *think* he was just saying this, the way we sometimes did to make Will feel proud of some baby accomplishment, but I couldn't be totally sure.

"Yeah."

"I genuinely didn't know you could do something like this," he said, tilting his head to one side. "Gracie, come in here!"

"No—don't get her," I said, but Dad shook his head.

I felt shy as soon as she walked in, even though it was Mom and she knew all about the painting.

"Yeah?" she said.

"Come look," Dad said, waving her over.

Mom joined us, and she studied it.

"The light—how'd you capture... That's really sophisticated technique, Lou."

I looked at the canvas again—I'd used the shadows and the white space to create balance, just the way I'd learned from the art books I had, just the same as Ms. Granger had taught us in art class.

"It's . . . it's incredible," Mom said, holding her hands to her mouth.

"It's official—we've got ourselves a miniature Georgia O'Keeffe," Dad said, using the booming tone he usually reserved for work or sports games.

"Go say good night to Will," Mom told Dad. She looked entertained by his little announcement.

"Great work, Lou. I mean it," Dad said.

I took a deep breath. Maybe with Dad gone, Mom would tell me the perspective was off again—I wasn't sure how to fix that with paint.

She took a seat on the couch, and I sat up and faced her.

"I'm so glad this is what you decided to do for your project," she said.

"Why?"

"If we'd made something together—something glass, like you wanted—it wouldn't have been all yours the way this is. I would have had to do it for you—you could only have told me what you wanted. But this is all yours."

I looked at the canvas again. Even if no one else would look at it and feel what I felt, I was sure that ten years from now, this painting would still capture what this year had been like for me.

～๑

"Wakey-wakey!"

I blinked.

I stared up at Dad and then let my eyes roll closed again. It was Sunday. I could go right back to sleep.

"Lou!"

"What?"

"Get up."

"It's the weekend," I said, rolling over in bed.

"We're going outside. I've got a surprise. Mom and Will are already getting bundled up." Dad stood at the foot of my bed. "Chop-chop!" he said, clapping his hands.

I kicked off my blankets and trudged behind him to the living room.

"What's happening?" I said.

Mom and Will were sitting on the couch in their parkas, the black pom-pom on Will's orange hat flopped down on the right side of his head. Mom had wrapped her green scarf around her neck a few times, and she was wearing a floppy gray hat that covered her eyebrows.

"You've gotta get dressed!" she said.

"Dad made us a skating rink!" I stared at a very perky Will and blinked a few times, still trying to wake up.

"What?" I said.

"Well, not exactly," Dad said, adjusting his hat.

"Well, then what?"

"A bunch of us at the firehouse decided to get a group together and clear off the pond at Plato Park for the week," he said, sounding a little proud. "We're going to take turns plowing it out so that the kids in the neighborhood can ice-skate. But we just finished, and we can be the first ones to give it a go—before anyone else."

"Go get ready! We're all set to go," Mom said, and the enthusiasm in her voice made me bolt back into my room to get changed. She was excited about going somewhere with us. For the first time since Nana died, it felt like Mom was excited.

∽

Once we'd reached Plato Park and put our ice skates on, I stood tall and surveyed the deserted scene in front of us. The morning sun was shining down, but the playground was still iced over. You couldn't even see the outline of the seesaw or the sandbox, just the snow-coated monkey bars and the swing sets towering over the rest of the park like monuments to the Freeze.

"Ready?" Mom said, and I nodded. She reached for my hand. Will was on her other side, and she stood between us like a buoy in the ocean, our navigator toward a safe path.

Dad was already standing on the ice, planted tall on the edge of the pond. He and the other firefighters had done a good job; there was a long section of clear ice for us to skate on.

"Let me do the first run," he said.

As he moved toward the center of the pond, I started laughing. He was basically walking on the ice, stumbling on every other step.

"He hasn't skated in years," Mom said, her voice low like a secret. She covered her mouth, but I could see that she was laughing, too.

From where we stood, he seemed to clunk forward

in this mechanical rhythm, the way a robot being controlled by a remote might. By the time he was almost at the far end of the pond, Will was laughing the hardest.

"Don't let him see you laughing," Mom said as Dad turned to look at us.

Dad gave us a thumbs-up. "All clear!" he called as he skated across the pond. He was looking back at us, instead of ahead of him. And he was headed right toward a tall steel garbage can that sat where the pond met the grass.

"Watch out!" Mom shouted, squeezing my hand so tight I had to rip it away.

I closed my eyes, cringing.

I heard a slam, and then a heavy thud.

When I opened my eyes, I could see Dad sprawled out on the ground and Mom flying across the pond toward him. I heard the crisp slice of her blades against the ice as she became smaller and smaller in the distance.

Will reached for me, but I couldn't look at him. My eyes were locked on Dad. He didn't seem to be moving.

Mom reached him, and I watched her bend down.

Her back was to me, but I could see her body shaking even from far away.

I grabbed Will's hand, still not able to look at him—I couldn't face the terror I knew would be in his eyes—and raced toward our parents. I was a better skater than Will, and I could feel his weight slowing us down. He was flailing, but I just kept moving, dragging him behind me.

Once we were close, I heard something that stopped me dead in my tracks: laughter.

I'd thought Dad was seriously injured, but as I took a closer look, I saw that the two of them were giggling.

Mom stood, still laughing, and held her hand out to Dad to help him up. He grabbed her arm, and her legs started wiggling. Her feet flew out behind her, and with a thump, she fell on top of Dad.

I skated toward them, ready to help pull her up. My arms and legs tensed as I glided over. I was afraid that Mom had run out of patience now, and she'd tell us it was time to go home before we'd even had any fun.

Mom was resting her head on Dad's shoulder. Dad's deep laugh seemed to stretch from his head to his toes.

Will shook his head. "What?" he demanded. This only made Mom and Dad laugh harder, infuriating Will.

Eventually, Dad hoisted himself up on his knees, and then used my arm to help him stand. He rubbed his back before helping Mom up, too.

Mom wiped the ice residue off her parka and her legs, and then she hugged Dad tight, right there on our makeshift skating rink.

～の

Mom was a showoff when it came to ice-skating. She moved so gracefully over the pond's surface.

She called out to me, "Come over here!"

We skated around the pond, hand in hand. It felt like we were dancing, the way Mom led us, and we fell into a rhythm.

The whooshing of the wind and Will's squeals as Dad twirled him around in circles on the ice were like the soundtrack to our routine, like we were figure skaters in the Olympics.

"This is the first time I've ever ice-skated outside in June," Mom said.

"And the first time we've ever had a whole ice rink to ourselves," I said.

"Courtesy of the Freeze," Mom said.

"*And* Dad," I said.

"*And* the rest of Firehouse Forty-Eight," she added with a little giggle.

～の

Eventually, Will got tired. He and Dad sat on a bench beside the pond while Mom and I kept skating. She held my hand, gloved fingers in gloved fingers, and we twirled around in semicircles on the ice.

I knew that soon we'd be cooped up back inside our apartment, but we weren't now. With each glide of my skates, each swish of metal cutting against the ice, I squeezed Mom's hand tighter.

Twenty-Four

In the days that led up to my time capsule presentation, I did my best not to think about it. There were other things that were harder to avoid thinking about, though. Nellie ignored me at school, and even though Priya *seemed* torn between us, she didn't sit next to me or look for me during recess.

Whenever I could, I hung out with Luke.

My ice-skating adventure with Mom gave me hope that Luke and I were making progress. It felt like she was finally popping her head out through a pile of heavy blankets; I could recognize her underneath the new parts that made me miss her.

When we focused on Luke's guitar playing and

perfecting Brian's song, I felt even more sure that the scene Luke saw in the ceiling was closer to becoming reality.

~ತಿ

The morning of my presentation, I woke up in a bundle of nerves, that dry-mouth, lump-in-my-throat, shaking-hands kind of anxious. I considered faking sick so that I wouldn't have to go, but Mom and Dad knew today was the day of the presentation; it wouldn't work.

On the TV in the living room, the *Wake Up, America* anchors were beaming.

I stared at the headline crawling across the bottom of the screen: *Sudden rise in temperature: Is a thaw on the way?*

I blinked, rereading the ticker message as it scrolled across the screen a second time. "What's going on? What's with the news?" I said, pointing to the TV.

"Oh, who knows? Don't read too much into it," Mom said, turning it off. "Better eat something." I followed her into the kitchen.

~ತಿ

On my walk to school, though, the headline tiptoed back into my thoughts. I kept my eyes peeled for signs of warming. The sidewalk was still covered in ice and snow, and the air was still cold, slithering underneath my layers like a snake to bite my skin. But the wind, while still howling, didn't cut as sharp against me as I walked.

Dad carried my painting for me in one of Mom's canvas protectors just to make sure I didn't drop it and get it all wet. Seeing him walk around with artwork hanging off his shoulder like some sophisticated painter would have made me laugh on any other day, but not today. All I could think about was what might go wrong during my presentation.

When we reached the school, I felt a crack on the sidewalk underneath me.

Will jumped up and down, and I stared at the ice beneath our feet. Each time the force of Will's body hit, the splinters of the crack grew. We watched as a little vein of water moved through the ice under us.

"See that?" Dad said, and he pushed the edge of the block of ice with the tip of his boot. "The layers underneath? They're melting."

I watched a second longer; the vein seemed to swim underneath us, still stuck inside the block. I wished I could stay and study it, but Dad handed me the canvas protector then, and my curiosity was replaced with dread.

He said, "Don't think about your presentation until right before, Lou. No sense. You're prepared. It's going to be just fine."

Easy for him to say—he didn't have to present his very personal time capsule artwork to a class that included a scary-intense teacher and two ex–best friends.

∿

When it was finally time for Ms. Lee's class, I slunk into a seat beside Luke and took deep breaths. He gave me an encouraging smile, but I felt too queasy to say anything to him.

Ms. Lee called on people to present in random order. Luckily, Candace Wu was called first, and I sank farther down into my seat.

After each completed presentation, as the next student was about to be called, I went through a cycle of fear, hope, and relief. Everyone's project was unique—if I hadn't had to present mine, I would have really enjoyed watching the rest of them.

Jamal had made a video of his favorite places covered in snow, and he'd drawn a cartoon of himself and held it up in the video. He'd narrated it all, telling us why he liked each spot. At one point, he held his cartoon self in front of a shut ramen restaurant with the silver gate locking the front door. His cartoon knocked on the door over and over again.

"Come back! I miss my ramen!" he said, using a goofy, high-pitched voice.

The whole class laughed, even Ms. Lee.

I laughed, too, but a second later I had a sinking feeling—my painting wasn't funny at all. Maybe it would make everyone feel miserable. I didn't know why I hadn't thought of this until now, when there was nothing I could do to change it.

With ten minutes left before the end of the day, Ms. Lee called my name.

I stood, my knees knocking together, and propped up my painting on a desk in the front of the room.

As I looked out at my class, I noticed that most

kids were staring at the clock or out the window. Maybe going right before the final bell of the day was best—no one would be paying attention, because we were all excited to go home.

"So, this is my project. I made a painting," I said. I stood to the side so that everyone could see.

"Great, Louisa. Tell us a bit about it," Ms. Lee said.

"Well, this painting represents what this year has been like for me. Originally, I wanted my mom to help me make this into a different kind of artwork. I wanted to make a glass sculpture," I said, pushing a piece of my hair behind my ear, "because in some ways, I feel like things are super delicate right now, like glass.

"But this is different. This painting is inspired by cave paintings in France that are from thousands of years ago. They're called the caves of Lascaux. They reminded me of our time capsule, because when you look at the paintings, you see what life was like a long time ago."

I took a breath; I could feel myself speeding up as I spoke.

"This painting tells you a little bit about what

this year was like for me. But I don't need to tell you what it means, exactly, because these symbols could mean one thing for me and something else for you. My mom told me that art should make you feel something, so I hope that's what my painting does, but I don't need to tell you what it should make you feel— that's up to you," I said, with a shrug that felt very awkward.

"Can we ask some questions?" Ms. Lee said.

"Sure," I said, despite the fact that opening things up to questions seemed risky.

"Andre," Ms. Lee called.

"I think I feel something when I look at this. It kind of makes me feel lost...or sad? Like you were having a really hard year."

I felt my body stiffen.

Of course, everyone would now know that while they'd all been having adventures in the snow together, or spending quality time with their family, I'd been stuck moping around in my apartment, my only joy coming from *Supermarket Sweep* and hot chocolate.

Andre continued, "It's kind of cool that when I look at that, I can see what you were feeling this year without you telling me, and I get it—it's what I was feeling, too, I think."

"Thanks," I said, surprised.

"That's great feedback, Andre," Ms. Lee said. "I think lots of us can relate to the idea that this year has been challenging, and disappointing, and probably not what all of us wanted it to be. I think your project, Louisa, isn't just a great use of symbolism. It's also an example of how art connects us, especially through tough times."

I thanked her, relieved that my presentation was over, and was getting ready to take my painting down when she said, "We have time for one last question... Nellie?"

I took a deep breath—*so close.*

If Nellie said something terrible to me now, in front of everyone, I thought I'd melt into the floor. I locked eyes with her and stiffened, wondering what she was about to say.

"This is a comment, not a question."

"Okay," Ms. Lee said.

"I didn't even know you could paint. It's really cool," Nellie said. "I get the feeling you're telling us something with the painting you can't say with words, but you can show us with your art."

I nodded, too stunned by her kindness to think of a response. After Ms. Lee thanked me, and the other kids clapped, I took my painting and put it back in its case near the closets, feeling a million times lighter. My painting had made other kids feel something—even Nellie had said so.

And I'd never have to present it again.

❧

After the last-period bell rang, I joined the line of students filing out of the classroom into the hallway.

"Lou?"

Nellie hovered behind me.

"I really *did* like your painting," she said, a little sheepishly.

"Thanks," I said, still a bit uncomfortable about her sudden niceness.

"It reminds me of your mom's sculptures."

"Really?" I said. I wasn't sure what had caused this sudden shift—why she'd decided to be so nice about my project after declaring our friendship over.

"I always thought it was so cool the way they

could make me feel happy, or sad, or confused, even when they were just, like, a vase, or a little figure," Nellie said.

She slung her backpack over her shoulder then, and I followed her out into the hallway. We stopped in front of a row of sixth-grade lockers, and she gripped the sides of the notebook she was holding tight to her chest. "I wanted to tell you—I *am* moving," she said. "I didn't want to leave and wonder if you hated me."

Even though we weren't friends anymore, hearing that Nellie was actually moving to Switzerland made me feel disoriented, like I was lost in my own neighborhood, trying, and failing, to find something that looked familiar.

"I don't hate you," I said, and I sighed. "And I was never *pretending* to be your friend. I don't know.... Things just felt different."

"They are." The sadness of her voice matched how I felt.

"But I could never hate you, Lou," and then, before turning and heading toward her locker, she said, "Everything's just changed."

On my walk home that day, I thought about my

painting reminding Nellie of Mom's work. Mom made delicate, beautiful things. It was a risk, trusting others with them. After sharing my painting, I thought I kind of understood why, for now, Mom wasn't making art: She wanted to hold her feelings inside, where she could keep them safe.

Twenty-Five

In the days that followed, I felt like a detective trying to discover even the slightest changes to our environment: mounds of snow that looked shorter, cracks forming in the ice under my boots as I walked home from school, the sun feeling warmer against my skin and shining longer in the day. I wondered if maybe Brian could have been right—were we going to have a snowless summer after all?

~⟋

That Friday, at our Makers Club meeting, Mr. Rojas told us that after we finished our Marvelous Metropolis project and it was judged, we could display it in the school library where everyone could see. Then, in his scraggly scrawl, he wrote a question on the board: *What adaptations do you predict our* Marvelous Metropolis *will have to make if the ice begins to melt?*

Andre was first to raise his hand. "We'll have to account for all the melting ice. We're not prepared to handle it. I don't think *anyone* has made a plan. What if everything floods?"

"Very interesting point. Anyone have any suggestions? What could people make to support us against flooding? What kind of materials would engineers use?" Mr. Rojas asked.

"What about if they made tunnels? That way if the snow melts and the streets flood, people could travel through those tunnels to reach each other," Luke said.

"That would be a great idea," Mr. Rojas said, and he wrote *tunnels* on the board underneath his question.

"What about if there was a way to collect all the melted snow and somehow clean it and reuse it?" Keisha said.

"I love that. Conservation! Not sure how that

would work exactly, but it's a great path to explore," Mr. Rojas said.

I sat, stunned, as I listened to this list of new challenges we'd have to face if the Freeze ended.

I leaned closer to Luke and said, "I didn't think that the Freeze ending would cause so many other problems. I thought it would just, I don't know, end, and things would go back to normal." I rubbed my palms on my jeans.

Luke gave me a sympathetic smile. "I'm not sure that things can ever really *go back*," he said. I knew he was talking about the Freeze, but I had this nagging feeling that maybe this thought applied to Brian, and to Mom, too.

I hated the idea of Luke losing hope in our plan. It made me feel incredibly alone, and I was silent for the rest of our meeting.

$\sim$

Will was building with one of my Lego sets at our wobbly kitchen table—not the kind for little kids, but a really complicated set with thousands of pieces. This one was a skyscraper. It was Saturday morning, and I was trying to finish my math homework before I went out to join Luke—he was getting obsessive about nailing Brian's song, and I wanted to encourage him, instead of accepting the opinion he'd shared during yesterday's Makers Club meeting.

I sat across from Will, working on a word problem.

Jin used 1/2 pound of blueberries and 1/15 pound of oatmeal to make 12 muffins. If he uses the same recipe to make 24 muffins, how much oatmeal is needed?

This seemed to be a pointless problem. I read it over and over again, becoming more confused each time.

"Hey, you two." Mom stood in the kitchen doorway.

She was wearing her work clothes: a gray shirt with paint on it and jeans with a hole in the right knee. It looked like she was getting ready to go to work at her studio; I got this hopeful feeling.

"I'm building a skyscraper," said Will.

"Nice, bud," Mom said.

Will's wavy bangs danced in front of his eyes as Mom ruffled his hair, and he nudged her away with his hand.

I thought Mom would be impressed with me for sharing my Legos with Will, but she didn't mention it. She opened the freezer, and I watched her stare into it for a minute too long. Then she took a package of some meat—probably chicken, like always—placed it on a dish, and moved it into the fridge to defrost.

"Mom?" I said.

She slammed the door to the fridge closed. "Yeah?"

"Are you going to work? Did you find a new studio?"

"What? Why would you ask that?"

"You...you're wearing your work clothes? And I know you've been seeming like—"

"I thought we were done talking about this—I'm not going to *any* studio again," she said, her voice sharp.

I watched her walk down the hallway to her bedroom and felt my eyes water.

"Are you gonna cry?" Will asked.

"No," I lied.

∽

That night after dinner, I stared down at my unfinished word problem set, overwhelmed. I couldn't focus on anything but Mom's attitude earlier, and how it made me feel a little hopeless for the first time in a long time.

I went downstairs to ask Luke for help with my math, and as I followed him to his bedroom, I saw Brian sitting on the couch in the living room, a folding table opened in front of him. He was writing something in a notebook.

"What's your dad doing?" I asked, once we were in Luke's room.

"His doctors want him to start journaling. He's written so many songs, they think maybe it'll be a way to spark some old memories or something—getting back into his old habits," Luke said. He didn't sound convinced.

He flopped down onto the floor. I sat opposite him, tossing my math notebook between us, and told him about the way Mom had snapped at me earlier.

"I thought the weather was finally getting warmer, so she was getting happier, and that made me think we were getting closer to the vision coming true," I said, my voice shaky.

"Maybe we are! It could just be that getting back

to glassblowing isn't a part of what's going to make her happy again," Luke said.

"Maybe," I said, but it wasn't just that she wasn't making art again. It was the way she'd snapped at me, and the expression on her face. She looked like she had before, when Nana had first died and she'd gotten that dazed, defeated look in her eyes. "What do you think I should do?"

"Well, you said she first seemed to be acting a little more like her old self when she started helping you with your painting, right?"

"Uh-huh."

"So why don't you start doing another one?" he asked. "Or ask her advice about a painting, or a drawing? And that will get her excited again. Don't force it, you know, not like your glass project idea. But just make it casual. You know, she could have just been in a bad mood."

I shrugged, hoping he was right.

ᔐ

The next afternoon, Mom had a different kind of project planned for us.

She'd laid piles of our laundry on her bed. My clothes and Will's were on opposite sides. We were supposed to go through the laundry, fold it, and if we saw anything we weren't going to wear anymore, put it in a pile on the floor for her to give away.

This was *not* the kind of project I enjoyed—I didn't want to spend my Sunday organizing.

Every time Will lifted a T-shirt out of his pile, he'd announce, "I forgot about this one!" before rolling it into a ball and putting it back on the same pile.

Mom had tried to correct this twice already. It hadn't worked.

"I was thinking," I said, holding up a shirt with the Eiffel Tower on it that I'd outgrown last year, "I really liked my time capsule painting."

"When do you get to bring that home?"

"Last day of school."

"I think we should hang that up. I know it's supposed to be something you don't look at for ten years or whatever, but it's really beautiful. And it's too big to hide or store somewhere, honestly," Mom said, tossing a brick-red shirt of Dad's into the giveaway pile.

"Okay...Well, anyway, I think I want to do another painting."

"Uh-huh," she said, clicking her tongue against her teeth and holding up a white blouse to the light.

"What do you think? What would be a good subject?" I said.

"Oh no! Moths! There are little holes in this," she said, examining the blouse more closely with her fingers.

"What?"

"Moths! I put those mothballs in there. They're supposed to protect against them." She sighed and tossed the blouse in the giveaway pile.

"Oh. Well, what do you think?"

"About what?" she said.

I was about to repeat my question when the doorbell rang. Mom dashed to answer it, and a minute later, she stuck her head back in the room.

"I've got to go handle a delivery downstairs," she said.

"What kind of delivery?"

"Just stay up here with Will. Finish sorting your clothes," she called, already halfway to the foyer. A moment later I heard the front door shut.

For a second, I considered obeying her. But there was something about the way she'd rushed to answer the door that made me too curious to stay put. I followed behind her, leaving the front door unlocked so we'd be able to get back in.

From our second-floor landing, I peered down through the staircase railing. Mom couldn't see me, but I heard her talking to someone. I recognized him: James, one of the sculptors who worked in the studio across from Mom's.

He patted a huge box, the kind you'd pack up if you were moving, and slid it closer to the doorway.

"Thank you so much for holding on to this. And for bringing it down here," Mom said.

"It was no problem at all. Rasheen and I miss you, Gracie," he said.

Then, with the slam of the door, he was gone.

I was halfway down the stairs when Mom noticed me. "I told you to stay with Will," she said.

"Why was James here?" I asked as I reached the bottom step.

"He dropped something off for me." She was holding the apartment keys in her hand, and she jingled them around, like she was nervous.

I leaned against the lobby wall and studied the large box. "What's in there?"

"Some of my pieces I'd left at the studio. The white-glove shipping people are going to pick them up now and send them out to a gallery in California to be sold."

"What's white-glove shipping?"

"They wrap and package the artwork safely to transport long distances," she explained.

"Can't I look at them before you send them off?"

"They're boxed up." She put her keys in her back pocket and rubbed her eyes.

"But this means I'll never see them again!"

She looked exasperated. "Louisa, you've never even seen some of these in the first place. The point of making my pieces is so that I can sell them. Don't make it a bigger deal than it is. Please."

"I'm not. I just want to see. Please?"

Her eyes softened, and she reached into her pocket, grabbed her keys, and cut the tape on the box open. "Just one or two—the ones on the top."

The pieces sat in bubble wrap, probably looser than Mom would have secured it, so it was easy for me to lift a tall sculpture out of the box and pull off the wrap.

It was the color of seagrass and as tall as the lamp

that sat on my bedside table, but way thinner. The glass was molded in curves that made the sides look like ripples in water. I ran my pointer finger along its side, and the curves felt cool against my skin.

"It's so beautiful."

"Thank you," Mom said.

"I think we should keep this one," I said, cradling it in the crook of my arm. "I think I'd call it *Tidal Wave*, maybe?"

"Louisa," she said, her voice full of no.

"It looks a lot like *Teardrop*, really," I said as I took a closer look.

"We can't keep *any* of them. I've agreed to sell them."

"But they're yours. I think we should keep all of them. I mean, what happens when things go back to normal and you want these back?"

"Louisa," she said, really slow, "there is no going 'back to normal' anymore. *This* is it. And this box: It's just sculptures, or vases, or little figurines. Just pieces. And when we sell them, we make money. It's just work."

"These aren't just *pieces*," I said, and I felt myself getting hot.

"Yes, that's all they are."

I hated the tired way she looked at me, like she'd given up.

I felt a knot at my core tangling tighter and tighter with all the lies Mom was telling herself, all the lies I'd told myself about why things were the way they were now. All I could do to make that feeling go away was to pull as hard as I could and snap the knot in half like an old rubber band.

"NO! Not to me!" I yelled. "They're more than just *pieces* to *me*! They're all I have to remind me of before!"

Mom stood up straighter. "Stop shouting! The neighbors will hear you!"

I reached into the box and started to grab as many of the pieces as I could fit in my arms—five—and hugged them tight to my chest.

"Stop it right now! STOP! Louisa! You'll drop them!" She put her hands out and tried to pull the pieces away from me, but I bolted toward the stairs before she could grab them. I could hear Mom following me as I ran up the stairs.

She was only a few steps behind me when she said, "Just stop, Louisa. Stop. We can talk about this. You've got to calm down."

I knew that if I stopped and walked back downstairs

with her, she'd put the vases and sculptures in the box and send them on their way to California no matter what I said.

I took the last steps to our second-floor landing two at a time, overwhelmed by the need I felt to save these pieces from Mom's own lack of interest.

What happened next felt like it went in slow motion.

Will swung our apartment door open, and the steel doorknob hit the wall with a smack. I jumped, shocked, and the vase I'd shoved on top of the others rolled off the stack in my arms.

I tried to reach for it, and the rest of them tumbled out of my hold.

Behind me, Mom shrieked.

The cold, shrill clink of glass breaking against the cement staircase echoed through the stairwell. Some of the pieces trickled downward from step to step before they shattered completely, prolonging the terrible chorus.

Will came over to me on the top step, and he peered behind me at the wreckage trailing down the stairs.

"LOUISA! What did you do?" he shouted.

Mom was still standing halfway down the staircase. Her face was gray, like she'd seen a ghost.

Just then, Luke's apartment door swung open and Alesha came running out.

"Oh. Whoa. Okay," she said as she walked up the stairs over the broken glass.

She held her hand out to Mom and guided her down to the ground floor. "All right. Everything's fine. You're all okay," Alesha said.

Once they were at the bottom of the stairs, Alesha turned back to me and held her hand up.

"Both of you stay. I'll come back. I don't want you getting cut," she said.

"I'm sorry," I said, but I wasn't sure if Mom heard. She disappeared with Alesha into her apartment.

I sank onto the top step and dropped my head into my lap. Will sat down beside me—he poked my arm until I lifted my head and looked at him.

"You didn't mean to do it, right? It's okay," he said.

I took a deep breath and tried to talk, but only a sob came out. I was old enough to know that it didn't matter if I meant it—I'd done something that wasn't fixable.

∽

After a few terrible minutes, I heard Alesha's door opening again.

"Louisa?"

I bent forward and peered through the slats of the banister. Luke was looking up at me. "Is my mom okay?" I asked.

He walked to the bottom of the staircase.

"Yeah. A little piece of glass cut her arm, but my mom cleaned it up. She just needed a Band-Aid. Come down," he said.

"I can't. Your mom told me to stay here."

He disappeared back into his apartment, and I wondered if I'd be sitting on the step until Dad came home from his shift, and would have to tell him that I'd broken everything and hurt Mom's arm.

Luke sprinted back a second later. "It's okay. She said to come down, but to be careful."

I took Will by the hand and guided him down the stairs, so that he wouldn't step on any glass.

"It's really not *that* bad," Will said, once we'd gotten to the bottom step.

Luke swallowed a nervous laugh.

~੭

Inside Luke's apartment, Alesha was placing a cup of

tea on the table beside the couch in the living room, where Mom was sitting.

"Are you two okay? Come, let's make sure you didn't get cut anywhere," Alesha said. Will bolted over to the couch and plopped down beside Mom. He stretched his arms and legs out, performing a quick inspection for any injuries. He checked the bottoms of his sneakers before saying, "All good!"

"Good," Luke said, sounding relieved.

"Come, I'll get you some water," Alesha said, beckoning for Will to follow behind her to the kitchen.

When he was gone, I walked toward Mom with shaking legs.

Luke stood behind me, and as I took a deep breath, preparing to face Mom, I got the comforting feeling that he was there to back me up.

"I'm sorry," I said. My voice sounded garbled, like peanut butter was stuck to the roof of my mouth.

"I can't talk about it. I just need…I need a minute," she said, her voice shaking.

"Okay," I said.

"Sometimes accidents happen, but at least everyone is okay."

That comment came from behind me. Brian was sitting in the armchair in the corner—I hadn't even noticed him. His voice sounded familiar, not as slow as it had when he'd first been injured, and it comforted me like a warm blanket on a cold night.

I found myself padding over to him, almost like an instinct; I felt safer beside him. I leaned on the edge of his chair. He looked a bit surprised that I was suddenly so close, but then he smiled up at me and said, "It's all okay."

He sounded very sure, and I decided I believed him.

Twenty-Six

The morning after the glass disaster, I stopped feeling like Mom's grief was something I could fix.

I lay in my bed as long as I could, after Will had gotten up and dressed. Eventually, Dad came to look for me. He sat at the foot of my bed and waited for me to say something, but I scrunched up into my pillows and kept my mouth shut.

When he realized I wasn't going to talk, he sighed. "I know Mom was really upset last night. That must have been scary for you."

He couldn't possibly understand. Last night had marked the failure of my mission. By trying to fix Mom, I'd actually made things much worse.

"She's not mad at you, you know. She knows you were just trying to help."

"No," I said, stretching my arms out in front of me. "I wasn't. I was trying to keep her vases and sculptures. And now they're destroyed."

My words came out feeling like arrows I was slinging at Dad, but he didn't flinch.

He just said, "Okay," and shrugged. "So what if they are? She was selling them, anyway."

"Yeah, for money. Now she can't even make the money for them, they're just gone, and I ruined everything."

Dad shook his head. "Louisa, things are replaceable. People aren't."

I knew that people weren't replaceable. That was the scary thing about them.

"Well, she's not going to replace *those* things. Ever. That's what she said."

"Forever is a very long time," Dad said, tilting his head.

After he left, I burrowed further into my bed. The only place I could go to escape was the ice house, but I didn't want to walk through the apartment and have to talk to Dad again, or face Mom at all. I wished I'd built a slide from my window right down to the entrance so I could be there whenever I wanted.

~⸰9

I would have hibernated in my room for the rest of the day, but eventually I had to get up to go to the bathroom. Besides, I knew that at some point, either Mom or Dad would force me to get ready for school. I opened the door only a crack and tiptoed down the hallway, hoping Mom wouldn't hear me, but when I opened the bathroom door she was standing at the end of the hallway, waiting for me.

The morning light streamed in from the window, and Mom's eyes glowed in the brightness.

"Lou, come here."

I obeyed, and she wrapped her arms around me and hugged me tight. She smelled like lilac soap and coffee, and I didn't want her to let go.

When she pulled away, she held both of my arms in her hands and said, "Yesterday was a bad day."

"I'm so sorry," I mumbled, looking down, but she cupped my chin in her hand and forced me to look at her.

"I forgive you. It was just a hard day all around, and we're not going to think about it anymore," she said.

"Okay."

"That means you don't get to feel guilty anymore. Got it?"

"I'll try," I said.

"Do you know how many pieces I broke when I was in art school?"

"No," I said.

"Way more than broke yesterday."

I wasn't sure I believed her, but I gave her a thankful nod anyway.

"Let's get you ready for school," she said, and I studied her, trying to figure out what seemed so different about her this morning.

Maybe *I* was different—maybe I'd finally let go and could see her clearly.

∽

"We have some good news, and some bad news."

Mr. Rojas had called an impromptu meeting of the Makers Club during our lunch period that day. He had sent a video tour of our model city to the judges' committee; I'd known right away that this meeting had to do with the contest results.

I stood in the science lab next to Luke, peering down at our model. When I looked up at Mr. Rojas, somehow I could tell he didn't have good news.

"I'll start with the bad news," Mr. Rojas said. "So, we didn't make it to the Marvelous Metropolis Final Three."

"What?" Andre said, outraged. "Why not?"

"Well, they sent a very nice email explaining that they were amazed by the number of problems the Final Three addressed. They provided real, practical solutions. Things like sanitation trucks, large-scale indoor farming for growing fruits and vegetables, things that people need immediately."

"But we solved our own *real* problems," Luke said.

"Exactly. I told you to think big, to figure out what would make you feel happy and good and right about living in a world where the Freeze was the future. You created a city that anyone would dream about living in—Freeze or no Freeze. You solved problems collaboratively, with creativity, and you made it beautiful, to boot."

"So then why aren't we finalists?" I said.

"Because the judges thought the other models presented more immediate solutions, and that's how they chose to evaluate the entries. And that's okay. Besides, we did win something."

"What?" Keisha said.

"Most Innovative City! Let me read you what they wrote.

> "We had so many entries, all taking different approaches to the problems presented by the Freeze. What stood out to our panel most about your Marvelous Metropolis was the way your team utilized the problem as a solution. Using ice and snow as integral materials for constructing a beautiful, thriving metropolis—complete with a pool, a beach, and a monorail!—represented a level of innovation that inspired us. Our panel feels confident in the future with innovators like your team as leaders. Job well done!

"You should all feel very proud. I know I am," Mr. Rojas said. "The way you found answers to problems that most adults haven't—it's what gives me hope for our future, too."

It was nice that our model gave Mr. Rojas hope for our future. I was proud of it, and I liked it, even if the judges didn't think we were worthy of being finalists. But from when we'd started the project in September to now, it wasn't just the grand prize I'd lost.

"Are you mad we weren't finalists?" Luke asked, once we were on our way back to the cafeteria to finish our lunch.

"Eh," I said, shrugging. "It didn't end up being what I'd wanted it to be in the beginning anyway."

"Well, let's face it. We are very innovative," Luke said, grinning.

"More innovative than those judges know, that's for sure."

∽

Our front walk was oddly squishy.

Luke, Dad, and I stood with our shovels, trying to figure out where to pile the slush. The mounds of snow on our front lawn had grown softer, almost gooey. Eventually we started shifting the goopy slush off the sidewalk—it sort of worked, but it was way messier than the crunchy snow we were used to shoveling.

"Let's do something fun for your dad's birthday, Luke," Dad said, once we'd gotten into the rhythm of slush-shoveling.

"Really?"

"Yep! Start of summer: Whether the Freeze ends or not, your dad is home, and that's something to celebrate."

"What should we do?" I asked.

"Well, I don't think it's going to be a beach day, *yet*," Dad said. "But…I don't know, I think the days of good snowballs are coming to an end. Might not be *too* long before we get a proper heat wave."

I wanted him to be right, but staring at him in his cap and boots, still surrounded by snow, it seemed unbelievable.

I dug my shovel into the snow then and flopped a mound of it behind me.

"Hey!"

"Sorry!" A big chunk of snow had landed right on Luke's head. It was seeping down his curls and onto his face like soapy shampoo.

"Hey. No laughing!" Dad said, and as we turned to look at him, he pelted us with snowballs.

∽

That Monday, I stared down at our Marvelous Metropolis model on top of the counter in the school library, its award ribbon and label affixed to the side of the big piece of clear plastic Mr. Rojas had put over it so that it would be protected.

"This is actually really cool."

I turned around and saw Priya standing behind me.

"Thanks," I said.

She took a step closer, so that she was standing next to me, and peered down to study the model. Afternoon light streamed in through the shades and made the green in her hazel eyes dance.

"You know, I didn't quit 'cause I didn't want to be friends anymore," she said. "I just didn't want to do *this* stuff anymore." She gave the case a light tap.

"That's okay," I said. "You could've told me."

"I wish I had," Priya said.

"Me too." I looked at her instead of the model. "I want you to know I was never just pretending to be your friend," I said.

"I know."

Maybe it was okay if all Priya had to say to me was that she thought the model turned out nice. Without Nellie there to anchor us, things probably wouldn't be the same between Priya and me, either.

"I've gotta go," Priya said a second later, and I nodded. She took a few steps toward the hallway before she stopped.

"Wait," she said, swinging her backpack to the side and rummaging around in it. She grabbed a book and handed it to me.

"I think you'd really like this. It reminded me of you," she said.

I looked down at the cover: *Rodrigo: Book One*.

I stared at Rodrigo's friendly face and smiled— he'd become so familiar to me in the past few months, but I'd still never bothered to actually read his books.

I thanked her, and as she left the library, I felt okay not knowing exactly how things were going to turn out between us. I could let the pages of our next chapter unfold, without rushing to sneak a peek at the ending.

Twenty-Seven

The next afternoon, Mom shuffled into my bedroom as I was reading *Rodrigo*. Once I'd started it, I couldn't stop. "Could you help me with something?" she asked.

"Fine." I followed her down the hallway to her bedroom.

"It's a little complicated."

"Huh?"

She stepped aside, and I stopped short when I saw a sheet of glass the size of our TV lying on the floor.

"Is this a new kitchen window? What's it doing here?"

"Oh. No. But that reminds me, I've got to follow

up with the super about that drafty old thing," she said. "But this, this is going to be something different. A mosaic."

She bent down. I saw now that there was a cardboard box at her side. She pulled out a piece of glass from one of the vases I'd dropped.

"You're making a mosaic?"

"I want to try something new," she said. "And I want you to help. Unless you don't want to."

"No! No, I want to help," I said.

"Well, roll up your sleeves! Let's plan this out."

∼๑

The next few days passed in a frenzy of news flashes and predictions and theories. The melting was unprecedented, but the snow had been, too.

"And tonight we are joined by Professor Mary Sato, who has been a voice of clarity throughout this period of uncertainty.

"What do you think this trend toward a thaw means for the Freeze? Is it safe to hope that we're moving toward an end?"

"Well, I wouldn't go that far. There's more research to be done before—"

"That's enough of that," Dad said, clicking the remote.

Mom and Dad were sitting on the couch, and I was helping Will finish a puzzle on the floor—it was mine, the Flatiron Building in New York, and there were way too many pieces for him.

"Hey! You've got to focus," Will whined.

"Got it," I said.

I searched for a piece of gray sky—I'd almost completed one section.

"I think, even if this isn't the thaw we've been waiting for, that'll be okay," Mom said.

"Huh?" I said, still searching for my missing puzzle piece.

"We've got everything we need right here," she said.

"Aw," Dad said, "that's so cheesy."

The two of them started giggling, and I just shook my head.

"Keep looking!" Will commanded.

"I am looking!" I said.

But I glanced back up at Mom and Dad, who were still laughing—sometimes they could be *so* weird. Will stopped his search for a missing puzzle piece and looked at them, too. A second later, he shot me a look that matched exactly how I felt: relieved.

June 28 was Brian's birthday. The day before had been the last day of school. Our summer break had finally arrived, but it didn't feel like summer. Not yet.

For the first time I could remember, we weren't going to the beach to celebrate.

But outside, things were changing. Melting had continued, and spread. The sun was staying out a little later every night, and the temperature was rising. There hadn't been any snowstorms in weeks—when there was snowfall, it was light and powdery.

Still, our ice house stood strong. The foundation was so thick that even though the snow around it was softening, the walls were still firm.

As Luke and I sat inside our house the morning of Brian's birthday, and I breathed in that crisp ice air, I had a gut feeling. I never liked my gut feelings, because they usually told me that something I dreaded was about to happen, or that I should do something I didn't really feel like doing—like be nicer to Will, or volunteer to help Dad with a chore.

But this gut feeling wasn't telling me to *do*

something—it was more like a message. Things were changing; the ice wouldn't last forever.

Luke reached into his pocket and held out a package of gum: a "minty-fresh" flavor.

"Want some?"

"Who got that for you?"

"The occupational therapist that comes for my dad. She gave me Peppermint Patties, too."

"No way!"

Luke reached into his other pocket and held a silver-wrapped Peppermint Pattie out to me.

"Thank you, thank you, thank you!" I grabbed it and tore open the wrapper.

Luke pulled another one out of his pocket for himself.

I took a tiny bite—I needed to make this last— and the sweetness of the chocolate and the coolness of the mint met in my mouth like old friends.

"It's so good," I said.

Luke laughed. "It kind of tastes like medicine if you ask me," he said, "but I'm glad you like it."

❦

After we finished our candy, we lay side by side on the ice.

I could hear Luke shifting the snow beside me to the same rhythm as my own limbs—back and forth, the sound of our puffy parkas brushing against the snow.

I closed my eyes, and when I opened them and fixed them on the ceiling, the image of my face shifted into focus.

Except this time, we weren't at the beach.

I was holding hands with Mom and Dad. Will was on Dad's other side. At first, I couldn't tell where we were. There were trees, and the sky was blue like an ocean wave. But then I saw the arch that stood at the gateway to Plato Park behind the four of us.

It seemed like we were just taking a walk, Mom and Dad meandering along the cement path—no snow in sight. I blinked and focused harder, wondering if I was missing something.

Mom stopped walking and pointed down beside her, at a plaque in the garden bed. She must have been reading about what types of flowers were growing.

Dad and Will were chatting in the background, but I couldn't hear what they were saying. I was standing beside Mom, waiting for her to return to our walking path. I didn't look impatient, the way I usually felt when Mom was slow with things. I seemed perfectly fine waiting.

When she did join me again, she reached for my hand. Her smile was soft, her eyes bright.

I felt like a piece that was missing had been found as I watched us together. But I wished I could take a picture in my head so I could save it to look at later—I didn't want this to be the last time I saw Mom like this. I wasn't sure what it meant, either, that we weren't at the beach and we weren't laughing or running around in the sun.

The vision faded. I wasn't sure how much time had passed, but it must have been a while, because when I turned back to Luke, he was sitting up.

"I saw something different," I said, pulling myself onto my knees.

"What was it?" he asked.

"It was still my family, but we were at Plato Park, and my mom was smelling flowers."

"How'd you feel watching it?"

"Uh, we all looked happy, but…"

"No, I mean how did you feel *now*, when you were watching it," he said.

I considered this. I'd always felt good during these visions, because in them, we all looked so much happier than we were now.

But today, I'd felt different. That moment between Mom and me, watching the look we shared—it made me feel calm down to my core.

"I guess...I guess, safe, maybe? Why?" I said. "What'd you see this time?"

"I was playing my dad's guitar, and we were in my living room. And then he started clapping to the beat, and my mom started clapping, too. I guess for the first time, watching it didn't make me feel like I was missing something. I just felt fine."

I played with the zipper of my parka. "So maybe we were seeing the future," I said.

He shrugged.

"Have you thought any more about your dad... your dad and the guitar?"

He looked very concerned at the question. "I've been thinking about something."

"Okay?"

"I think I should play the song for my dad today. And just see what happens."

"What do you think might happen?"

"I'm not totally sure, but...I just...I think it's time to find out."

"I think so, too," I said, but inside, I feared what might go wrong.

~o

That afternoon, we headed down to Luke's for Brian's birthday party.

Alesha cooked Jamaican food, and the whole apartment smelled like garlic and ginger. It made me hungry right away. Over dinner, Mom and Dad's conversation with Brian was all small talk, like he was a stranger instead of practically family. I tuned them out and talked to Luke about Rodrigo—I'd let him know that I'd started the first book, and he was practically dancing with excitement. Will chimed in with irrelevant questions that made Luke and me roll our eyes.

After dinner and cake, we all sat around in the living room. Our parents talked about the warmer temperature—it was all any adults talked about now—but my eyes were fixed on Luke.

He looked very nervous—he kept pulling at the long sleeves of his shirt.

"I'm going to do it," he whispered, and then, before

I could say anything, he stood up and moved closer to our parents on the couch.

"I wanna play you a song," he said.

All four parents looked surprised, but also amused. I sometimes used to put on little performances for my parents: songs, dances, skits. I couldn't imagine Luke doing that, ever.

Alesha straightened up so that she was giving Luke all her attention. "That would be excellent," she said. "Some entertainment!"

"Go for it, Luke," Dad said.

Luke walked over to the stand in the hallway where Brian's guitars rested, picked up the one he'd been practicing on, and carefully placed the strap over his neck. I watched as he stood in front of everyone, his eyes fixed on the floor. He snuck a peek at Brian, but only for a second.

I started shaking a little. Luke took a deep breath, and I could hear his rattling exhale.

"Wait!" he said, right before I thought he was going to start. "Your drums!"

I shook my head. "It's okay," I said. "Go ahead."

"No. Go get them. Please?"

"Sure," I said.

I bolted out of their apartment and up the stairs to ours, grabbed my drums off the floor of my closet, and ran back down the stairs, panting. The whole time, I pictured Luke waiting in awkward silence.

"Back!"

Luke was standing with the guitar, tapping his feet, when I flew back in. I took a seat beside him on the floor with my drums. I looked up at him and waited until he started to strum.

"*Lyin' awake, the door slammed behind you,*" Luke sang, his voice shaky. He was staring right at Brian, like he was singing the song just to him.

After thirty seconds of playing along with Luke, I stole a look over at Brian. His mouth was moving, but it was hard for me to hear him over Luke's strumming.

Dad looked at Brian, too.

> "*When you look at me across the room,*
> *We don't have to say a word to each other—*
> *You sit next to me and I make room.*
> *Those carefree days have faded to blue,*
> *The color I think of when I think of you.*"

I could hear him. We all could.

Luke's guitar playing became less and less steady. He was mesmerized, watching Brian sing. The look in Luke's eyes was so familiar—the exact same look he'd had when he'd watched the ice house ceiling.

"*But I'm looking back and since I don't know when...*" Brian trailed off and stopped singing as quickly as he'd started, his mouth shutting like a snapping turtle's. Luke's smile faded.

Something inside me welled up, and I knew I had to keep the beat for us both. I restarted my steady drumming and kept going until Luke heard the beat. He looked over at me like he'd woken up from a dream. He began to match my rhythm again, like he had during all of our practices.

Then I heard Dad's voice, hoarse and slightly off-key: "Whoa-whoa-whoa-whoa."

Alesha and Mom joined in, too. Mom started clapping her hands, keeping the beat with me.

Brian's eyes flickered as he realized they were singing his song to him. He started clapping then, too, and I kept on drumming until the beat matched the excited rhythm of my pulse.

I hadn't seen Luke's vision, but I couldn't imagine a scene more perfect than this one.

I tried not to let my mind wander to my own vision, and why it hadn't come true.

~⁙~

Later, our parents took chairs out to the backyard and set them on the patio. They sat there while Luke, Will, and I ran around in the slush.

"It's almost warm," Mom said.

It wasn't really—only about forty degrees—but compared to the constant barrage of frigid air, gusts of wind, and harsh hail, I understood what she meant.

She stood up and walked to the edge of the patio.

I watched, wondering if she was going to say something about the ice house.

But instead, she looked up at the sun.

She stood right in the path of its rays, and the warmest smile spread across her face. She closed her eyes and stayed like that a minute. Then she looked over at Dad and me and started laughing—a real Mom laugh.

Will, Luke, and I played tag for a little while, because Will begged us. He kept chasing us, even after we'd both given up on running fast to get away.

"Luke?" Brian was waving to Luke, and Luke

hurried over to him. I used this as an opportunity to stop our game of tag and followed Luke. Will called out after me, annoyed that we'd given up his game, but I ignored his whining.

"What's up?" Luke asked. He seemed a little nervous as he looked at Brian.

"Can you give me a guitar?"

Luke shot me a confused glance, and then he looked to Alesha for permission.

"Sure. Go get it, Luke," she said, with a quizzical look in her eyes.

A minute later he came back with one of Brian's guitars and handed it to him. Brian wrapped his fingers around the neck of the guitar and plucked at the strings.

Everyone fell silent; even Will stopped his whining.

Brian strummed for a minute, the strings releasing an awkward, out-of-tune sound, almost like a squeaking violin. I heard Luke's sharp inhale.

I regretted ever suggesting that Luke let Brian try to play—I didn't even want to watch this.

But then, just as I began searching the adults' faces to see if someone would interfere, the awkward notes stopped.

"I scared you for a minute," Brian said, a playful spark in his eyes, and for that split second, he looked just like the Brian I'd always known. "I guess I'm a little rusty."

After that, we all seemed to relax. Brian strummed a few melodies—mostly in tune, and for the first time in so long, we were all together the way we'd been so many times before.

This time was different, though: It felt like a dream come true.

Twenty-Eight

The sun streamed in bright through the blinds in my bedroom, but I heard hail pelting against the window. Hail on July 1—I would have been shocked, but the Freeze had taught me to stop trusting the weather people.

I sat up in bed to take a closer look, just in time to see a pebble hit the pane.

Still half asleep, it took me a minute to connect the pebble to the yard below me, and when I looked down Luke was waving up at me.

He motioned for me to come downstairs, and I gave him a thumbs-up.

Outside, Luke was wearing his coat, but it wasn't buttoned, and he had no gloves on. I'd grabbed my sneakers instead of snow boots on my way out, and as I stepped into the icy slush, my sneakered feet sank. It was disgusting.

I trudged through the sludge to get closer to Luke, who was standing in the middle of the yard.

"What's going on?"

"We can't just let it melt," he said, staring at our ice house.

The warm weather had finally gotten to it—the sides were softer and were sloping inward.

"I don't think we really have a choice," I said.

"No. I can't just watch it melt away."

"So what do you want to do?"

Luke reached into his jacket pocket and pulled out the keys to the shed.

I followed behind him. Inside the shed there were yard tools, measuring tape hanging from the ceiling, toys spilling out of a box in the corner: my old Hula-Hoops, a jump rope, a volleyball, and some baseball bats leaning against the wall.

I watched him eyeing the bats. "What do you think?" he said.

I picked one up and ran my fingers along the smooth aluminum.

"I think this will do it," I said.

"If you don't want to, we don't have to. We can leave it alone," he said.

"No. You're right. We should be the ones to say when it's over."

Back outside, we stood side by side in front of our house.

"It wasn't going to last forever," Luke said.

"Right. It was supposed to melt one day," I said.

We stared at each other, and then back at the house: a silent agreement.

I took a giant step forward and whacked at the front wall with my bat. I'd expected a terrible, harsh sound—like metal against glass.

Instead, there was a pop, like punching your fist through a cardboard box, and the front wall folded into the center.

Luke was holding his hand to his mouth. I let the bat hang down at my side. His laughter startled me for a second, and then it didn't.

Of course. It had seemed way more dramatic to us than it actually was: It was already melting.

I started laughing, too.

Luke lifted his bat into the air and leapt forward, swinging his arm down and shouting, "Hi-*ya!*"

In the end, it took only about ten hearty swings of our baseball bats to totally demolish our house.

The layers of snow and ice that covered the yard seemed to absorb the blocks of the house so that they were barely even noticeable—just a few big chunks of ice like a tree stump that seemed to say *we were here.*

We sat on the back stoop and stared out at the snow.

Neither of us said anything for a while. The air was warm; the sun was shining bright. It was strange, having my coat unbuttoned and not freezing.

Luke reached into his pocket. "I forgot," he said, and he slid the piece of *Teardrop* into my hand. "Found it in the snow."

I hadn't looked for it, or even thought of it, busy with all the demolition, and I felt a pang of panic at the possibility of having lost it.

"I'm surprised it didn't shatter when we were hitting all the ice," he said.

I closed my hands around it, filled with gratitude.

"Thank you," I said. I thought of Nana—the view from her piano bench, the glimmer in her blue eyes, and the lilt of her voice. All the pieces I'd lost, in the one I held now.

And then, right after Alesha called us inside for breakfast, I said, "I'll miss it a lot."

"Uh-huh," he said. "But you know, even though our house is gone, we *do* still share a building."

"That *is* true," I said.

"And now we have a lifelong secret—one no one else would ever believe."

"I wouldn't have believed it if it hadn't happened to us," I said.

"I would have."

"I know," I said, smiling a little. "But you know something? I kind of don't think it was magic anymore. I think it was sort of like a North Star, shining light to get us here."

"I like that," he said. "But...where are we, exactly?"

I felt the sun's warm rays tickle my nose, and I looked up at the sky.

"Home," I said.

Acknowledgments

Deepest thanks to my brilliant agent, Steven Malk, for providing me with your wisdom and guidance every step of the way. Your thoughtful advice has meant more to me than you'll ever know and has been a calming influence on this first-time author. I feel incredibly fortunate that you took a chance on me.

Many, many thanks also to Andrea Spooner, my extraordinary editor, for your great care, thoughtfulness, and understanding throughout this process. From our first conversation, I knew Louisa and I were in the best hands. Your insights and advice helped to shape this book in countless ways, and I will be forever grateful.

Thank you to my copy editors, Annie McDonnell, Anna Dobbin, and Barbara Perris, for your attention to detail, and to Esther Cajahuaringa, Siena Konscol, Christie Michel, Jenny Kimura, and the rest of the amazing team at Little, Brown Books for Young Readers.

Thanks to Wendy Sabrozo, Courtney Longshore, Andrea Morrison, Hannah Mann, and all of the dedicated members of the wonderful team at Writers House.

Tom Clohosy Cole, you so perfectly captured the magic of *The Ice House*. It's a dream come true to have your illustration grace my book cover.

To my dearest friends Elyse Chu, Nadia Kale, Liz Raynor, Elizabeth Teel, and Linda Wu—thank you for your love, understanding, enthusiasm, and support. Your friendship has made me feel blessed beyond measure. I've been fortunate enough that many more friends have been with me along the way than I could possibly list here. You know who you are, and I thank you.

To my entire family, thank you for being the best audience, no matter the story.

Mary Kate, thank you for being my first writing teacher. You've never failed to give me encouragement, inspiration, and support. Thank you also for being my oldest, truest friend. I'm incredibly lucky to have a sister like you.

And from the bottom of my heart: thank you to my parents, Tom and Nancy Sherwood. Every day I am grateful that I grew up in our home, surrounded by books, with you two as my parents. Thank you for always encouraging and believing in me. Mom, thank you for always listening. I hope one day I can be half the storyteller you are. And Dad, thank you for always honoring my bedtime story requests, and for all the trips to the library.

Book Club Discussion Guide

1. How does Louisa try to "fix" her mom? How does Luke try to "fix" his dad? Do you think it's their responsibility to "fix" their parents? Why or why not?

2. Louisa and Luke both experience a trauma in their family. In what ways do their families respond to these traumatic events similarly? In what ways do they differ?

3. What does Louisa's teacher Ms. Lee mean when she says that "one fact can be interpreted in two totally different ways" (page 15)? How is this statement true in the novel? How have you seen this in your own life?

4. Louisa's nana took Louisa's interests seriously, even though she was a kid. Who in your life takes you seriously, and how do they show it?

5. Luke observes that "adults have to have an explanation for everything" (page 149). What does

he mean? Do you agree or disagree? What are some things you have wanted adults to explain or solve that they haven't been able to adequately?

6. Mr. Rojas encourages his students to try to solve real-life problems affecting their world. Do you believe kids can make a difference? What are some real-life examples?

7. Louisa gets frustrated that there isn't a single, definite explanation for the Freeze. Why is not knowing so hard? How does Louisa's mom offer solace about such uncertainty? What are some situations in your own life where you struggle with uncertainty?

8. Why are Louisa and Luke ambivalent about returning to in-person school? How do you feel about remote schooling versus in-person schooling?

9. How do Louisa's friendships with Nellie, Priya, and Luke shift during the Freeze? Have you ever outgrown a friendship? Do you think Nellie or Louisa could have handled their feelings in a more constructive way?

10. Throughout the book, Louisa begins to feel closer to Luke than to Nellie and Priya. Why do you think this is? What are some examples of moments where Luke was a good friend to Louisa? What do you think

Louisa learns about friendship throughout the book? What qualities do you think make a good friend?

11. Why do Louisa and Luke think the ice house is magic? How are music and art "magical" in the novel? Do they ever feel magical in your own life?

12. Louisa uses symbolism for her time capsule project. What does the ice house symbolize for her? What does it symbolize for Luke? What might it symbolize to you, or to the novel as a whole?

13. How does the Freeze compare to and contrast with the COVID-19 coronavirus pandemic? How do the families' experiences of living with global stress and change seem similar or different from those you might have witnessed or lived through yourself?

Nancy McGuinness

Monica Sherwood

grew up on Long Island and currently lives in New York City. She is a former elementary school teacher with a master's degree in Childhood and Special Education from Hunter College and currently works in educational technology designing digital products for teachers and kids. Monica began dreaming up *The Ice House* during a particularly long, cold winter, inventing a world "where snow and ice came to represent that desperate feeling of being hopelessly stuck in one place ... but where change is, eventually, inevitable."